# RICH LAWYER, POOR PRIEST

I0623792

BY CANADIAN AUTHOR AND RETIRED LAWYER

DONALD W. DESAULNIERS

# RICH LAWYER, POOR PRIEST

E-Book ISBN:  978-0-9920653-5-5

Paperback Book ISBN:  978-1-987888-16-4

This is a work of fiction. All characters, locations, organizations and events are either a product of the author's imagination or used fictitiously.

Any resemblance to any persons, living or dead is purely coincidental, with one exception.

Jim Corbett, who died in 2002, was the best friend of the author, and Jim's name has been used as a fictitious character in this novel as a tribute to a true gentleman who was in real life that rarest of rarities, a totally honest and caring lawyer.

# ABOUT THE AUTHOR

Donald W. Desaulniers is a retired Canadian lawyer from Belleville, Ontario. He ran his sole practitioner legal practice there from 1973 when he was called to the bar in Ontario until he retired in September of 2009. The author graduated in 1968 with a B.A. from University of Waterloo (Majoring in Philosophy) and in 1971 received his LL.B. from University of Western Ontario Law School.

He still resides in the beautiful city of Belleville with his lovely English wife, Jane and their cat.

The author began writing fiction as a hobby shortly after he retired and enjoys writing about the legal profession. He has published more than 100 novels exclusively on Amazon but still feels that RICH LAWYER, POOR PRIEST is his best novel even though he wrote it in 2013.


NOVEL SERIES ABOUT LAWYERS

SLIMY LAWYER (#1 in Series)
SLIMY SUES AMERICA (#2 in Series)
SLIMY GETS SHAFTED (#3 in Series)
SLIMY GETS DISBARRED (#4 in Series)
SLIMY TASTES THE GOOD LIFE (#5 in Series)
SLIMY LAWYER CHECKS OUT (#6 in Series)

VANISHING LAWYER (A WORLD WITHOUT ME)
VANISHING LAWYER #2 (UNWANTED WITNESS)
VANISHING LAWYER #3 (FUGITIVE ALIEN)
VANISHING LAWYER #4 (SAVING THE PRESIDENT)
VANISHING LAWYER #5 (SWINDLING SENIORS)
VANISHING LAWYER #6 (SAVING TRUMP AGAIN)

WEIRD LAWYER #1 (NOVICE ATTORNEY)
WEIRD LAWYER #2 (TOUGH TIMES)
WEIRD LAWYER #3 (A PINCH OF JEALOUSY)

THE WRONG LAWYER (#1 in Series)
SNARKY LAWYERS (#2 in Series)

<u>OTHER LAWYER NOVELS</u>

CARJACKED LAWYER (A Travel Nightmare)
LAWYER HEAVEN
THE LAWYER AND THE PRINCESS (A Love Story)
REVILED LAWYER
FEISTY OLD LAWYERS (Biting Bureaucracy))
THE LAWYER WHO HATED MONEY
STUBBORN LAWYER (A CANADIAN MYSTERY)
DISCARDED LAWYER (BUT NOT DEAD YET)
LOCKDOWN LAWYER
FAILED LAWYER, POMPOUS ANGEL
SHUT THAT LAWYER UP
LUCKY LAWYER
PARADE OF DEAD LAWYERS
LOVING THE LAWYER, LOATHING THE LAWYER
THE LORD SNATCHES AWAY
LADY LUCK LOVES LAWYERS
THE CHRISTMAS LAWYER
RICH LAWYER, POOR PRIEST
TERRORIST LAWYER
THE LAWYER'S MUSLIM NEIGHBORS
FAKE LAWYER
NAIVE LAWYER
THE TWIN SHADOWS
THE CHEAPSKATE TWINS
BUYING REDEMPTION
REVENGE DELAYED
LAWYER IN THE TOILET
CELESTIAL COINCIDENCE
BROKE, DISGRACED AND ALONE

A RETIRED LAWYER'S DOOMED ROMANCE
THE LIPPY LAWYER'S ROMANCE
LOVE SEDUCES A FOOL
TEMPTING THE GOOD LAWYER

## ROMANCE NOVELS

THE LAWYER AND THE PRINCESS (A Love
Story))
JOBLESS CHRISTMAS (A Travel Romance)
BEVY OF BEAUTIES (Finding Love After Loss)
SWEET ROMANCE BACK HOME

## ACTION NOVELS

ELUSIVE WITNESS (Hard to Kill)
STARTING OVER (Danger in Missouri)
LADY INJUSTICE (Falsely Accused)
UNQUALIFIED DETECTIVE (A Financial
Mystery)
TRAILER PARK REVENGE (Crime Thriller)
DIE NOW OLD MAN
CROSSING A RICH MAN (Turning the Tables)
VILE FAMILIES
THE LEFT TACKLE'S CHRISTMAS
ESCAPE FROM EVERYTHING
MARTY MARCOTTE'S REVOLVING LIFE
FIFTY YEARS LATER (Hitchhiking in Donald
Trump's America)

## TY WARD ACTION/ADVENTURE SERIES

TY WARD HITS AMERICA (#1 in Series)
TY WARD'S HOLIDAY FROM HELL (#2 in Series)
TY WARD'S NEXT WAR (#3 in Series)
DEADLY WITNESS (#4 in Series)
A YOUNG HOOKER'S THANKS (#5 in Series)
TY WARD'S NEXT WAR (#6 in Series)
TY WARD'S SHATTERED PEACE (#7 in Series)

TY WARD'S ROUGH JUSTICE (#8 in Series)
TY WARD'S LOCKDOWN RESCUE (#9 in Series)

## WARD JONES ACTION SERIES

WARD JONES #1 (Fledgling Predator)
WARD JONES #2 (Damsels in Distress)

## UNDERCOVER HILLBILLY ACTION/MYSTERY SERIES

UNDERCOVER HILLBILLY #1 (A Financial Mystery)
UNDERCOVER HILLBILLY #2 (Murder Suspect)
UNDERCOVER HILLBILLY #3 (A Stinking Mystery)
UNDERCOVER HILLBILLY #4 (Another Strange Mystery)
UNDERCOVER HILLBILLY #5 (Missing Half-Brother)
UNDERCOVER HILLBILLY #6 (Dangerous Adversary)

## SUPERNATURAL/SCIENCE FICTION NOVELS

ALIEN SPECTATORS
FAILED LAWYER, POMPOUS ANGEL

HAUNTED FUNERAL HOME #1 (Gorgeous Ghost)
HAUNTED FUNERAL HOME #2 (Ghost Detectives)
HAUNTED FUNERAL HOME #3 (Irrational Guilt Trip)

## YOUNG ADULT NOVELS

CELESTIAL COINCIDENCE
MYSTERY OF THE OLD DESK
YOUNG BUT NOT STUPID

## NOVELS WRITTEN UNDER PEN NAME "LANCE MAJESTIK"

COLD CASE LAWYER
UNDERCOVER TRUCKER (An American Mystery)
OLD MIND, YOUNG BODY (Body Switch)
UNVACCINATED OLD LAWYER (Rebel Without a Jab)
BETTER TIMES (A Comeback Story)
LOVE IN OLEAN (An American Romance)
CRAZY OLD LAWYER (A Talking Skin Tag)
LOVE MOCKS A LIMP DICK (War of the Sexes)

## NOVELS WRITTEN UNDER PEN NAME "DURWARD GARBAGE"

TRIPLE GARBAGE (Three Short Novels)
WRONG PLACE, WORST TIME
ABANDONED ALIEN (Space Aliens for Donald Trump)
GOLDEN CHAOS (Stock Market Meltdown)
NASTY MAN (Mr. Jerk)
ALMOST A LAWYER
SQUANDERING MY FORTUNE
REVENGE FROM HER GRAVE
LAWYER ON THE RUN (Panhandling Attorney)
SCORNFUL FAMILY (Eating Insults)

# TABLE OF CONTENTS

CHAPTER 1 (Rich and Greedy)

The annoying grey fur ball had jumped up
on my lap, shedding its revolting hair all
over my expensive black pinstripe suit.

Showing remarkable self-restraint, I
resisted the powerful urge to grab the little
weasel and hurl it against the stunning curio
cabinet at the far side of this huge parlor.

The quickest way into any old woman's
purse was by way of her beloved pet, so I
forced my face to break out into an angelic
smile while my hand lovingly stroked the
disgusting hairy pest.

For a moment I lost my train of thought as
I struggled with the quandary of how to hide
the pending dry cleaning tab onto the old
lady's legal bill. There was no way I'd ever
brush off this growing fungus of cat hair
using just my lint brush.

I commanded myself to focus on the task at
hand, namely getting old Miss Powers to sign
her new Will and Power of Attorney.

For the past thirty minutes I had been
fielding a legion of tough questions from the
old bitty and I was now genuinely concerned
that she was going to bail out on me and
refuse to name me as her sole Estate Trustee
and Power of Attorney.

If that happened, then the boatload of
easy money I hoped to earn when the gullible
old fool died would be flushed right down the
crapper.

My client was seated on a beautiful
antique loveseat facing me. I was on a
matching chair with the bundle of grey vermin
now irritatingly settled on my lap.

1

"Fluffy certainly seems to like you, Mr. Billingsworth," she gushed. "That's the one important matter that I felt had no place in my new Will. If I consent to employing your services to look after my affairs both before and after I'm gone, I need to feel assured that Fluffy will be well taken care of. He's been my constant companion for the past nineteen years. What will become of my little darling when I die or if I get seriously ill?"

Law school never taught us how to act but I realized from the tone of these questions that if I ever needed to give an Oscar winning performance, this was the time.

The blatant lies literally poured out of my slimy mouth.

"Jean, you don't have to worry about a thing. No matter what happens to you, Fluffy's happy future is assured. I adore cats and I live alone in an apartment right above my office. Fluffy and I will make a cozy little team if a time ever comes when you're unable to care for the little darling."

For added effect, I scratched behind the weasel's ears which fired up a humongous purr from the little beast.

My masterful performance brought a huge smile to Jean's wrinkled old face and a tear to her eye.

"I'm so relieved to hear you say that, Mr. Billingsworth, and I'm now fully satisfied that I've chosen the right lawyer. Please invite your secretaries in and we can complete the formalities."

My long-time secretary, Florence and her useless fifty-four year old daughter, Lana were the required two witnesses, and they had been patiently waiting outside in Florence's car for my signal. I hadn't wanted them overhearing my conversation with Jean.

I gently eased Fluffy off my lap and walked to the front window where I gestured to the ladies to come into the house.

A few minutes later Jean Powers was all signed up and my secretaries left to return to the office.

Just as he had done from the moment I entered Jean's Victorian mansion, the detestable grey fur ball continued to follow me like a fawning disciple.

I stooped down and gave the beast one final petting just before I departed.

As I backed out of the driveway, old Miss Powers stood beaming in the front window while she waved at me like I was royalty.

My job here was done.

I waited until I had driven around the corner and was completely out of sight before I snarled aloud, "Look what you've done to my best suit, you despicable little weasel. I'll have you put down the minute the old bitty is dead."

That outburst made me feel significantly better.

As I made my way back to the office, my chest puffed up with pride. I still had the uncanny ability to exude sincerity and trustworthiness.

Allow me to introduce myself.

My name is Boyd Billingsworth and I've been a lawyer in Belleville, Ontario for the past forty-one years, my legal practice now being restricted to Wills and Estates.

My reputation in the community was impeccable.

In my humble opinion I deserved a lifetime achievement award for maintaining such a solid standing in spite of my penchant for swindling widows and their close relatives, those unclaimed treasures otherwise known as spinsters.

Both groups were the world's easiest marks and the finest source of cash flow that any attorney could possibly wish for.

I likened myself to a farmer lovingly tending his crops. I meticulously planted the seeds of trust by regularly attending church services and various church-sponsored activities where I presented myself as the world's most caring lawyer. Eventually a fine crop of little old ladies miraculously bloomed seeking my sage legal advice and thereby giving me the opportunity and distinct pleasure of harvesting their money.

In reality I was a selfish, miserly predator, greedy to my very core, but my public persona was just the opposite.

I've been blessed with all the physical attributes required to play the role of the wise, honest and compassionate lawyer.

My full head of naturally wavy hair was an incredibly distinguished mixture of silver, grey and light brown, a genuinely artistic masterpiece.

I was the perfect height, a couple of inches over six feet with a slender build. There was absolutely nothing threatening or unsettling about my appearance. In fact I could have been the poster boy for what most people imagined a kindly and modestly successful small town attorney should look like.

Add to that powerful visual image my other great asset, being the gift of perfect verbal delivery, and the result was diabolically potent. My deep voice resonated with distinction and was never tarnished with distracting pauses or stammered words. I could read out a recipe for lasagna and make you believe from the tone of my voice that I was imparting for your ears alone the secrets of the universe.

I've learned to fake the aura of absolute sincerity, and my prey, the numerous widows and spinsters present in this rapidly aging society, have no realistic chance of preventing me from sharing in their wealth.

It's a rare week in which I was forced to work more than twenty hours and the old dears kept dying like clockwork, creating a steady stream of obscenely lucrative fees.

In most cases I was even able to double-dip my greedy paws into these vats of wealth. The money I earned for being the Estate Trustee was enormous enough, but then I was able to grasp a sizeable bit more by handling the legal work on those same estates.

Possibly my clients were not indicative of your average oldster, but it was very unusual for me to process an estate worth less than a million bucks. Many were substantially larger and my standard trustee fee of 5 percent literally stuffed my pockets with easy money.

It's been more than twenty years since my income has been less than half a million dollars. I was a real stickler for figures and by my precise calculations, last year's income worked out at a somewhat eerie $666 for each hour worked.

Even more remarkable, my office overhead was astonishingly low. I did all my own accounting records, partly because I greatly enjoyed doing so, but also to keep prying eyes out of my personal affairs. Similarly, I prepared all my own annual financial statements and did all my own tax returns.

My current and only secretary, Florence, who had been with me for over twenty years, was almost eighty-two but still needed to supplement her government pensions with part-time employment. Her daughter, Lana, or as I called her under my breath, Lana the leech, hadn't been willing or able to keep a job since she was in her early twenties. She had been living for free off her hard-working mother for at least thirty years.

In order to assist Florence a bit, from time to time I threw a bit of work Lana's way like I did today when I employed Lana as the second witness for Jean Powers' legal documents. I paid Lana well for the bit of time involved. Both ladies did what I told them and kept their noses out of my business.

Despite my being filthy rich, a frugal upbringing had rendered me completely incapable of spending freely. The bulk of my money had been invested with an elite specialty bank in Ottawa, so no one in Belleville had any inkling of my true wealth.

It was almost noon by the time I got back to my decrepit office building, a century-old former funeral parlor which had served as my place of business during my entire legal career.

For the past twenty-five years I've also lived in an apartment on the top or second floor. My law office had always been on the main floor.

My intense thrift had limited the building upgrades to zero and proper maintenance to an absolute minimum.

I've always adhered to the philosophy that it's cheaper in the long run to postpone repairs until something actually breaks. As a result, the current state of my building was rather forlorn.

I had convinced myself that the upside, in addition to the monetary savings, was that the shoddy appearance of the building completely masked my financial acumen and gave the distinct impression that I must be honest and charged only the fairest of legal fees. The gullible public would expect a highly successful attorney to operate out of a palatial office.

How wrong people could be!

Divorce had blasted most of my fellow lawyers at one time or another in their careers and severely curtailed their wealth, but I was one of the lucky ones.

My one and only wife, Gabriela, with whom I did get along remarkably well for almost ten years, had the courtesy to develop cancer and die long before the ravages of time would have inevitably caused our marriage to deteriorate.

Fortunately, we had no children.

Gabriela's bittersweet demise had occurred way back in the fall of 1987 and I was devastated for a year or two, throwing myself full tilt into my law practice.

I was wracked with guilt for the horribly selfish relief I felt knowing that my precious assets had been spared the possibility of marital confiscation that a divorce virtually guaranteed.

The horrendous hours I worked diverted my mind away from the loneliness and depression that Gabriela's absence had spawned.

The steep increase in my income resulting from that heavy workload was a bonus I didn't really appreciate until years later.

To my credit, I had remained completely faithful to Gabriela ever since. In all those ensuing years, I had not dated even a single time.

Money had replaced Gabriela as the love of my life.

CHAPTER 2 (My One and Only Friend)

Florence was just locking up the office as I arrived. She only worked mornings. I went up to my apartment and made myself a quick sandwich.

Then I walked the two short blocks to my bank and put Jean Powers' original signed Will and Power of Attorney into my safety deposit box.

While at the bank I purchased some American cash for my upcoming trip to Las Vegas. I already had ample traveler's checks left over from my previous holiday.

Back in the office, I toiled for a couple of hours ensuring that everything was shipshape on the estates I was currently administering. I concluded that no one would miss me over the next two weeks and that meant that I could truly enjoy my time off.

Nothing ruined a holiday like last minute problems at the office.

I phoned my one and only friend, Jim Corbett, a former law school classmate who had operated his own law practice here in Belleville since we had both set up our offices in 1973. Jim had retired more than ten years earlier because of failing health.

He was also a widower and was five years older than me. Jim was very close to housebound in his modest two-bedroom condominium. We had been best friends for more than forty years.

Jim was the only person in town with whom I let my true nature flow out. With everyone else I maintained a fake aura of sincerity and probity.

Corbett could smell my bullshit a mile away and was never shy about calling a spade a spade.

As a result most of our conversations entailed the trading of insults which I suppose was therapeutic for both of us.

"It's only me," I began when Jim answered. "Is there anything you need me to pick up?"

Jim had an extensive list of groceries for me to get as well as two cases of beer. Usually I shopped for him on Saturdays and then we'd get drunk at his place each Saturday night, but this week we were meeting on Thursday night since I was heading off on my trip on Friday morning.

He ended the conversation by barking, "Don't get any of that no-name crap this time. I want name brand food even if it costs a bit more. The same goes with the beer. That garbage you found on sale the last time tasted like cat's piss. I want Molson Export Ale and nothing else."

"Yes, boss," I teased as we hung up the receivers.

I cooked frozen fish and chips for supper and then went shopping for Corbett.

After dropping off the groceries and beer at his place, I drove back home, checked the office answering machine for messages, of which there were none, and walked the two miles back to Jim's condo.

We liked to drink beer during our visits and I never drove even if I'd had just one or two drinks. There was no quicker way to ruin one's reputation than getting nailed for drunk driving.

I was way too cheap to spend seven bucks on a taxi cab, and hoofing it there and back cost me nothing and kept me slim.

It was almost eight o'clock by the time I reached the condo and Jim already had a beer in his hand and an empty on the small table beside his chair.

"You started without me, you hopeless lush."

"I was afraid you'd drink my place dry before you headed off to get raped by the slots. Besides, even I can't stomach listening to you drone on about how rich you are unless I've numbed my brain with alcohol. Did anything interesting happen today?"

I told Jim about the feline pest that wouldn't leave me alone at old Jean Powers' house. He found the situation most amusing given my intense dislike of cats.

"You haven't told me anything about this Vegas trip, Slimy, other than you'll be gone until the 19th."

Corbett insisted on calling me by the nickname he gave me years earlier when I first began bragging about swindling little old ladies. At the beginning I was mildly insulted but had grown to rather like the nickname. Don't ask me why.

"I'm really looking forward to the time off. You won't believe the bargains I got on the internet by being patient and booking at the optimum times."

"I bet there's some catch to every so-called deal," Corbett interrupted. "Don't leave out any pertinent details. Start with your flight."

"Flying out of Toronto was never in the running. The airport taxes are just too high, so I'm leaving from Syracuse as usual. I booked the trip several months ago when one of the airlines offered a fantastic deal. The return flight was only $215 Canadian including taxes. That's the second best price I've ever snagged."

"I bet it's not a direct flight," Corbett snapped.

"Of course not," I barked right back at him. "You can't fly direct from Syracuse to Las Vegas."

I was unable to suppress a grin.

That was a dead giveaway to Corbett who used to be an excellent poker player, and he pounced.

"You're not telling me everything, Slimy. I can read you like a cheap novel. How many stopovers do you have to suffer through?"

"None of your drunken business," I fired back as I stood up to fetch myself another beer.

Jim asked me to get him a refill while I was up, and then, like a dog with a bone, he persisted with his interrogation, but I was just as stubborn in refusing to divulge any further details.

Finally he managed to get my goat by intimating that the airline had somehow shafted me and that I was too embarrassed by my stupidity to confess that I had been taken.

"You never learned how to spot true value, Patsy," I spat out in frustration.

That was my equally insulting nickname for Corbett, based on his incurable gullibility during the entire time he ran his law practice. Jim was a soft touch for every loser and beggar in town. If he hadn't given away so much of his money to anyone with a sob story, he'd be able to live like a king now.

"If you're too embarrassed to admit how many stopovers you've got, at least tell me the departure time from Syracuse and the arrival time in Vegas."

I saw no harm in revealing that bit of information, so I replied.

"My flight leaves at six o'clock Saturday morning and I'll arrive in Las Vegas at nine-thirty in the evening, Vegas time."

"I don't believe it," Corbett blurted out as he broke out laughing.

I could see his devious little mind calculating something and after a moment of reflection he pounded his hand on the arm of his chair.

"Pathetic! It's going to take you more than eighteen hours to travel what should be no more than a five hour trip. How much would it have cost you to fly direct from Toronto?"

"If I'd timed it perfectly, I could have booked it for $405."

"You're insane," Corbett moaned as he threw his hands in the air.

He proceeded to haul his carcass off the recliner and limped over to a nearby desk where he located a calculator. Corbett tapped away for a moment and then glared at me with a sneer on his fat puss.

"You're spending an extra thirteen hours in order to save $190. That works out to less than $15 an hour. You brag about ripping off your clients and earning over $600 an hour. You could recover what you're saving in less than twenty bloody minutes at the office but instead you're willing to suffer through an exhausting travel ordeal. How can you possibly justify that? You sit here smirking like you've pulled off some sort of genius heist. Can you even explain your warped reasoning?"

"As usual, Patsy, you can't see the bigger picture here. This is personal time and is in no way, shape or form related to work. Open your small town mind for a moment while I let

13

you in on the sheer brilliance of my travel arrangements."

"This total bullshit I've got to hear," Corbett retorted.

"First off, Corbett, your calculations are total garbage. You forgot to ask about the return trip home, which involves another eight hours of extra travel time. In all I'll be enjoying twenty-one hours of extra but scintillating time getting there and back, so that reduces my savings to just over $9 an hour."

"Are you demented? That's even worse. Face it Slimy, you've just proven that you're an idiot."

"You're still missing the point, Jim. Not only am I saving $190 in pure personal profit, but I also get to see several extra cities for free."

Corbett almost spat out his mouthful of beer in his haste to rebut my perfectly valid point.

"Rushing around a bunch of airports to catch connecting flights isn't some form of exciting sightseeing adventure," he bellowed. "One airport looks exactly the same as another."

"To your untrained eye, perhaps, but I enjoy watching people and soaking up the flavor of each city. There's another possible bonus lurking in the background with my unique elongated method of travel."

"Like having a heart attack caused by the anxiety of running from one gate to another in a stressful panic," Corbett interjected.

"That exercise actually keeps me healthy. No, what I'm talking about is the chance of getting bumped and scoring a huge payday. Don't you remember from your own trips long ago? The airlines are always asking for volunteers to catch later flights in exchange for substantial compensation. I'm an absolute expert at taking advantage of those lucrative opportunities. With even modest luck, I might wind up flying free. Under the right circumstances the airlines might even have to pay me handsomely to fly if the remuneration they offer is more than the price of my flight. Face it Patsy, I've discovered a way to beat the airlines on their own home turf."

"Talk about false economy," Corbett groaned. "You'd risk losing your hotel reservation in Las Vegas for the dubious thrill of arriving a day late and losing some of your precious vacation time. Surely you realize that the hotel will still charge you for the night you missed. How do you possibly consider that to be saving money?"

"I've got it all worked out," I grinned. "I've booked a room in Las Vegas with guaranteed late arrival for just Saturday night and it only cost me $23. I consider it nothing more than cheap insurance. If I arrive as scheduled, then I've got a place to stay. If I get stranded somewhere at the airline's expense, they normally allow at least $100 for a hotel room. I can elect to take the cash and sleep on the floor in the airport for free if I feel so inclined or I can take the substitute room. The meal allowance money I'd get would more than make up for the lost twenty-three bucks. I've created a guaranteed win-win situation for myself."

Corbett's jaw hung down in sheer bewilderment as he attempted to comprehend what I explained.

Finally he muttered, "But it's your holiday. How can you put yourself through all that crap when it means you'll have less time to enjoy yourself in Las Vegas?"

"The entire experience constitutes my holiday, not just the period in Vegas. I find that scoring a travel compensation deal is just as exciting as hitting a decent slot jackpot and it's far more likely to happen. The one-armed bandits are incredibly tight these days. That's one of the reasons I go for two weeks now. There's always the hope that I'll score a lucrative deal with the airlines and spend some well-compensated time in a mystery city. It still leaves me with plenty of time to lose my gambling budget in Sin City."

Corbett still couldn't fathom the logic buried in my reasoning.

Eventually we changed the subject and spent the rest of the evening reminiscing about the old days.

At eleven o'clock I said my drunken goodbyes and staggered back to my own apartment.

## CHAPTER 3 (The Holiday Begins)

Friday morning dawned. Strangely enough, I didn't have a hangover from last night's drinkathon with Corbett.

I worked in the office for an hour and left Florence to man the fort for the next two weeks.

An expensive automobile is nothing but crack cocaine for losers who are so plagued with self-doubts that they crave a visible status symbol.

Only a moron would throw good money into a luxury vehicle. Drive it off the lot and you've already lost tens of thousands of dollars.

Not to mention that a prestigious car automatically sports an invisible bumper sticker screaming "ROB ME, I'M RICH". The low-lifes of this world can read that slogan loud and clear even if the owners of the expensive vehicles are oblivious to the message that they're publicizing.

As a result, my own car is a black 2002 Chevrolet Cavalier. Sure, it has received a few dings from careless cretins throwing their doors wide open in crowded parking lots, but I didn't obsess each time I noticed another blemish.

I named my beauty "Little Chevy" and its absolute mundaneness also served to accentuate my honesty to the public. Surely a rich shyster attorney would be driving a top of the line Mercedes Benz or BMW. This fellow in the old Chevy must be a straight shooter.

Image is so much more important than substance.

The lack of internal features had little or nothing to do with portraying my desired image. That was solely a product of my intense frugality. Although Little Chevy had automatic transmission, there was no air conditioning, heated seats, GPS or any other of the outrageously costly enhancements suggested by the slimy dealers to extort even more money out of naïve car buyers.

As soon as I departed the Belleville city limits, a sense of naughty freedom flooded over me.

My role playing was put on immediate hiatus.

For the next two weeks my mouth could hurl insults at anyone and everyone who displeased me in the slightest way.

Now I could release the inner asshole that was imprisoned within me but kept totally subdued in my hometown.

I drove along Old Highway 2 all the way to the casino near Gananoque and stopped there for a bite of lunch.

Afterwards I felt like risking a few dollars on the Caveman Keno slots before continuing on to Syracuse.

Those machines weren't where they had been the last time I had stopped here a year or two ago. I spotted an attendant at the refreshment stand.

"Where have you dolts hidden the Caveman Keno machines?" I barked at the young guy.

"I'm so sorry sir, but we no longer have them. There are other keno slots near the front door."

"What games are on those machines?" I asked belligerently.

"I'm pretty sure they only have regular keno, Triple Trouble keno and three-way keno, sir."

"Those games all suck," I replied in disgust. "What bozo decided to get rid of the Caveman slots?"

The kid cringed at my rudeness but disappointed me by holding his temper.

"It wasn't me, sir. Our boss said that those slots were getting old and we couldn't get replacement parts any longer."

"Well, then you won't be stealing my money any longer either," I snarled. "If you can't keep your customers happy then you may as well close this place. Your damn slots get tighter every time I set foot in this dump. You bastards have picked my pocket for the last time and I hope this shit-hole goes belly up."

With that pronouncement I marched off and returned to my car, pleased that I had found an opportunity to be obnoxious to a stranger so early in my vacation.

Twenty minutes later I was crossing the Ivy Lea Bridge heading into the USA.

Despite an urge to sass the border guard, I resisted. There was no point aggravating someone with the power to make my life miserable.

I stopped at Adams, New York and filled up with cheap gas. It amazed me how the Yanks complained about high gas prices when their fuel was a real bargain compared to Canada.

When I reached Syracuse, I located my hotel after a bit of searching. It wasn't particularly close to the airport and was in dire need of upgrading. I had never stayed there but a fellow cheapskate had bragged about what a great bargain it was. The place wasn't even listed on the internet so I had made the reservation by telephone.

The room rate was a most reasonable $49 and that also enabled me to park Little Chevy there for free while I was away. Since I wasn't certain if I'd make it back to Syracuse late in the evening of April 19<sup>th</sup>, I hadn't booked a room for that night.

While I was checking in, the useless young desk clerk was intimidated by my aggressive demeanor and didn't have the authority to guarantee me the same room rate if I decided to stay over whichever night I flew home.

I made him summon the assistant manager who, after I badgered him mercilessly for a few minutes, consented to my demands. I made him give me the rate guarantee in writing. Any lawyer worth his salt knows the joke that a verbal agreement isn't worth the paper it's written on.

The hotel didn't have its own restaurant so I treated myself to supper at a place just up the road, where I feasted on the nightly special of a tasty salmon steak, baked potato and a glass of water. Soft drinks and booze are far too costly in most diners and I refused to pad the owners' pockets by paying their outrageous beverage prices.

Back in my room I drank three cans of American beer from a six-pack I had purchased at Adams when I had stopped for gas.

I went to bed contented at ten o'clock.

The hotel wake-up call startled me at four the next morning. I had been dreaming that I lived in my apartment with ten dirty, destructive cats, and my new pal Fluffy was just in the process of puking on my sofa when the telephone thankfully released me from the nightmare. The stench of cat vomit was still vivid in my mind as I quickly showered and dressed.

The free hotel shuttle whisked me and several other guests directly to the airport.

My first flight was right on schedule. It was a short but full connection to Newark, New Jersey. I walked around that airport checking it out, never having connected there before.

For once Corbett was right, though. The inside of all airports, just like casinos, looked pretty much the same.

The next flight was to Atlanta, Georgia and it lasted almost two hours. Again the plane seemed to be full but no pre-flight announcements were made about it being overbooked.

There was a two hour wait for my next connection to Houston, Texas. By now I was hungry since I had eaten nothing so far today except the paltry package of free peanuts provided on the second flight.

I grabbed a personal pan pizza and Pepsi at a fast food outlet near my departure gate.

So far this journey was beginning to disappoint. There remained only two opportunities to score some freebies from the airlines.

This third flight was about half an hour late leaving and the plane wasn't even full. I noticed at last half a dozen empty seats.

We gained an hour by entering Central Standard Time but my ass was beginning to get sore by the time we touched down at George Bush International Airport in Houston.

A rather lengthy three hour wait now loomed before the final leg of this trip would take me to Las Vegas.

For one reason or another I hadn't spoken with anyone on the flights so far and, disappointingly, no opportunity had presented itself to be rude to anyone.

CHAPTER 4 (Rich Lawyer, Poor Priest)

I arrived at Terminal B and checked the overhead information board. My final flight would depart from Terminal E and was expected to be on time.

As I began walking toward the TerminaLink train area, a gentleman about my age with snow white hair and wearing a Catholic clerical collar spoke to me.

"Excuse me, sir. Do you have a moment to help me find my flight information?"

Immediately my devious mind perked up. At last an opportunity to be an asshole was presenting itself.

I stopped and pointed at the logo on my casino shirt.

"What does this say?" I asked with a deadpan expression on my face.

The priest looked at me oddly but leaned closer to read the words.

"It says 'EL CORTEZ HOTEL AND CASINO. WE PRODUCE WINNERS'," he replied politely.

"Exactly," I responded sarcastically. "It doesn't say 'AIRPORT STAFF', now does it?"

Having driven my point home, I swirled around triumphantly and began walking away.

"I'm so sorry, sir. I must be dyslexic. I didn't mean to misinterpret the writing on your shirt. Will you give me a chance to interpret it accurately?"

That bizarre reply stopped me in my tracks. Curious, I walked back to the priest to find out what he meant.

He peered closely at my shirt and then glanced up since I was several inches taller than him.

"Now I fully understand your comment, sir. I did misread it. Do forgive me. I thought it

22

said 'WE PRODUCE WINNERS' but now I realize that it's just a clever code which translates into 'WE PRODUCE POMPOUS BOORS'. I certainly won't pester you again."

This time it was the priest who abruptly turned his back to me while he looked back up at the flight information screen.

I broke out laughing. The little pervert had bested me in my own rudeness contest.

"You win," I joked. "How can a lawyer possibly hope to insult a priest and get away with it? You get all the best comeback lines handed down to you directly from the man upstairs. Let's start over. How may I help you?"

The cleric turned back to face me. He evaluated me for a moment to ensure I was serious and then said, "I can't find my flight on this board."

"Which flight are you looking for?"

"I don't see Las Vegas Flight 402 with United Airlines."

I glanced up at the screen.

"What time is it arriving?"

"It's not. I'm flying on that flight to Las Vegas," he answered.

"That explains why you can't find it. You really do have difficulty with reading comprehension, don't you? What does it say at the top of this information board?"

The priest looked up and saw the huge word "ARRIVALS". He looked at me blankly and then the penny dropped. He smiled.

"Departure information is on the other screen over there," I teased.

"In my defense, this is the very first time I've ever been in an airport. The past few days have been dreadful at my parish and I'm a bundle of nerves right now. I expect that explains why I was rude to you just now. I'm so sorry."

"Forget about it. I deserved it. I enjoy acting like an asshole around strangers when I'm on vacation. Back home I have to be on my constant best behavior. Let's find your flight information."

We walked over to the departure board and quickly located Flight 402. I pulled my boarding pass out of my pocket and realized it was also my flight.

"You're on the same flight as me and it's departing from Terminal E, Gate 17, presumably on time. Do you have your boarding pass yet?"

"No, I didn't realize I needed one. I've got my airline ticket."

"That looks like one of the United service counters down the hall. Come with me and I'll make sure you get what you need."

There was no line-up as we approached the attendant.

I took charge.

"Hello, ma'am; I've got Aisle Seat 28C on your Flight 402 to Las Vegas. My friend here requires a boarding pass for the same flight. Do you have a seat anywhere near mine?"

"Let me see, sir. Why yes, we do. Window Seat 28D is open. That's the advantage of checking in so early."

"That's wonderful," the priest exclaimed. "I've never flown before and a window seat would be fantastic."

After the woman handed the priest his boarding pass, I said, "There you go, Father. You're all set. Just make sure that you get to the correct terminal and gate on time and you'll be just fine. I'll see you on the plane."

A stunned expression suddenly filled his face as he stammered, "Would you mind terribly if I tagged along? You seem to know your way around airports and I have no idea how to navigate my way to Terminal E."

I felt devilish.

"You don't intend to stick to my ass like some annoying hemorrhoid, do you?"

The priest's entire face turned the most intense shade of crimson.

I let him wallow in embarrassment for a moment before I continued.

"I thought priests were trained to see the truth right through any veil of bullshit. I'm teasing you. Of course I don't mind your company. Do you want to get something to eat in this terminal or wait until we get to Terminal E?"

Again the priest seemed ill at ease.

Finally he blurted out, "I'm humbled to admit that I'm on a very strict budget. Would you mind terribly leading me to Terminal E? Then I can sit at the gate while you have your meal."

"I've got a better idea. I'll take you to Terminal E but then I'll treat you to supper there. It'll be my personal penance for jerking your chain earlier."

We walked together to the tram station and caught the train to Terminal E. It was standing room only and quite hectic.

"I don't think I could have found my way here without your assistance," the priest commented.

We selected a small diner, ordered a modest supper at the counter and found an empty table.

"Please forgive my tardiness in introducing myself. I'm Father Timothy Camacho and I'm a Catholic priest from a tiny and very poor rural parish at the extreme east end of south Texas."

He extended his hand, which I shook.

"I'm Boyd Billingsworth, a lawyer from Canada. It's nice to meet you. Las Vegas is a strange destination for a man of the cloth. You haven't absconded with this month's collections, have you?"

Of course I meant it as a joke, but Father Timothy turned beet red again as he blurted out, "Oh, my goodness, no; what a dreadful thought! I assure you that I've paid every cent out of my own paltry savings."

"I'm just teasing, Tim. We lawyers are sick puppies. Where are you staying in Vegas?"

"I haven't reserved anything yet. I plan to telephone one of the Catholic churches when I arrive there and hope that they'll put me up for free in one of their facilities."

"That sounds a bit risky to me. What will you do if they can't or won't accommodate you?"

"Perhaps I should have called ahead, but at my parish we've always welcomed visiting priests. I expect it's no different in a large city. We're all one big Catholic family."

"Good luck with that," I retorted.

"I'm sure that God will look after me even though I'll be in a strange city. I'd guess that this isn't your first visit to Las Vegas."

"You're right. In fact this will be my eighty-sixth trip to Sin City."

"That's shocking! Do you have some form of hideous gambling addiction?"

I laughed out loud.

26

"I thought priests were supposed to be kind and tactful. What kind of a loaded question was that?"

Timothy blushed yet again.

"I'm so sorry. Forgive my impertinence. It's so uncharacteristic of me. It must be the excitement of this whole travel experience that's causing me to blurt out rude questions as if I were an impulsive teenager. I really meant no offense."

"It's not possible to offend an attorney. I'm no addict. In fact I could be the poster child for responsible gambling. I set firm limits which are totally affordable, and I'm an incorrigible cheapskate on top of that. I'm afraid the casinos don't have much chance of putting their greedy hands in my pockets to extract my cash. I just happen to love travelling and Las Vegas is my favorite destination. Believe it or not, Vegas is a very inexpensive place as long as you control your gambling and avoid the Strip."

"I'm relieved to hear that. My vacation budget is extremely limited, I'm afraid."

"How much money did you bring with you?" I pried.

"Very little, I'm embarrassed to admit. I haven't taken a vow of poverty but my salary from the church is very modest."

"Don't evade my question. How much money did you bring with you?"

"I've got just over $200. My return flight is paid for but I ran into an unexpected expense yesterday and was forced to forfeit most of my vacation spending money. Paying for this trip had already drained my meager bank account and I don't have a personal credit card."

"How long will you be staying in Las Vegas?" I asked.

"My flight back to Houston is next Saturday morning."

"Then you're pretty much doomed. You can't survive on thirty bucks a day. You won't be able to attend any shows or take any tours, and gambling is completely out of the question. Why did you even bother to come?"

"My flight was non-refundable so I didn't feel as if I really had any choice. Just seeing the city will be enough of a thrill. I don't need to lavish myself with costly entertainment."

"Our flight won't arrive in Vegas until at least nine-thirty tonight assuming it departs on time. What will you do if you can't reach anyone at the church at such a late hour?"

"I'm sure God will look after me."

"It doesn't sound like He's done much of a job so far. What was the emergency yesterday that cost you most of your savings?"

"I think I'd rather keep that information to myself, especially since you appear to be something of a skeptic."

"I'm crushed. I haven't missed church on a Sunday back home in years. Sometimes I take in two services on the same day. What kind of skeptic would attend so regularly? Tim, you've got me pegged all wrong."

I didn't add that the only reason I went to church was to troll for new widows to fleece. There's no better place to meet rich elderly women. Often I took in the morning service at my own United Church and then went hunting at one of the many evening services at other denominations. Quite often I even hit a Catholic mass on Saturday. I considered myself to be an equal opportunity predator.

I smiled as I recalled how the lawyers at those other churches guarded their widows and spinsters like a vicious male lion protecting its pride. It took great patience and skill to wrest a rich old girl away from her own family lawyer, but my refined appearance and smooth tongue had successfully snared many a new client from the clutches of my horrified competitors.

Father Tim was as gullible as my buddy Corbett. Again the priest apologized for his rudeness when I was the one blatantly prying into his personal life.

Then he launched into a pathetic explanation.

"One of my most vulnerable parishioners, a wonderful lady with two children and a deplorably lazy and drunken husband, was about to be evicted and tossed out of their rented home. The county refused to step in and even threatened to put the kids into foster homes if they didn't have a roof over their heads. Maria came to my church begging for help but our poor box was empty and there was insufficient time to seek emergency financial assistance from the diocese. I saw no viable option, so I used my trip money and negotiated with the landlord to let the family stay. He accepted my $1,200 in full satisfaction of the rental arrears plus May's upcoming rent. That's why I'm so short of cash as I begin this vacation. I had expected to secure an inexpensive motel once I arrived, but now I'll simply rely on my church to put me up."

"That's an admirable story. How long have you been a priest?"

"The thirty-ninth anniversary of my ordination will be later this month during the Easter celebrations."

"That's interesting. I was called to the legal bar in Ontario just over forty-one years ago. How long did it take you to become a priest?"

"In all I completed nine years of post-secondary education."

"My God! That's even more schooling than I had to endure in order to become a lawyer. I'm sixty-six now. How old are you?"

"I'm sixty-four."

I decided to get outrageously personal in order to get a rise out of the priest.

"How much money did you earn last year?"

Father Tim eyed me curiously for a moment before replying.

"If I disclose that information to you, will you reciprocate?"

"Sure, although you might be better off not knowing."

"My salary is $14,000 annually plus I receive free use of a car and a free but tiny apartment at my church. The IRS values those benefits as an additional $6,000 of income. Now it's your turn."

"I made just over $600,000 last year."

"I presume that you're spouting off your gross earnings before the usual business overhead. How much were you actually left with?"

"That's a very astute comment, Tim, but in fact the figure I quoted was my net income after my office expenses were paid but before taxes. My office overhead is extremely modest, amounting to about $60,000 most years. Income tax is a bitch in Canada but at the moment I'm even able to keep my effective tax rate very low by using a professional corporation to stash most of the profits."

"I presume you must work horrid, stressful hours in order to amass such an obscene level of income," the priest commented petulantly.

"That used to be the case until I restricted my law practice to estate work. Now I only work about twenty hours a week and I'm able to take off eight or ten weeks a year on holidays. What kind of hours do you put in for your salary?"

"I guess I'm perpetually on call so it's not really possible to answer that question precisely. Do you mind if we change the subject? For some reason I find your revelations quite disturbing."

We had finished our meals anyway and there were people waiting for empty tables, so Tim and I made our way to our gate area and found seats right near the United counter.

"How long will you be staying in Las Vegas?" Timothy asked.

"I'm booked there for two full weeks. I fly back home on April 19th."

"Do you have a preferred hotel when you travel there?"

"I tend to shop around for the best rates. I'm actually staying at three different downtown hotels on this trip. Tonight I'm booked at the Las Vegas Club for just the one night. Tomorrow I move over to the El Cortez for seven nights, and then I'm at the Plaza for the last six nights."

"I've read a bit about Las Vegas but I didn't realize that there was a downtown area. Is that just another name for the Strip?"

"No, the Strip is where all the massive and expensive hotels are. It's too hectic and way too pricey for my frugal tastes. The downtown area has about ten hotels all compressed in a fairly small area, so it's easy to get around. I assume you've heard about the light show called the Fremont Street Experience. That's in the downtown section of Las Vegas. I generally hit the Strip once or twice during my trips just to walk around and see what's new."

"How do you amuse yourself for two solid weeks?" the priest asked.

"Mostly with the underage hookers."

Father Tim turned crimson again and his jaw dropped. I didn't even crack a smile as he stared at me unable to mask his shock and horror.

Finally I broke into a grin and explained, "That was a joke, Tim. Sorry to pull your leg again. I've got a bizarre sense of humor which I can't use back home, but on my holidays I can let my true self out for a run. In actual fact I spend my days walking around, watching people and playing the slots. In the evenings I like to listen to the free bands and watch the outdoor light shows."

"That's certainly a relief, Boyd. I didn't know how to respond."

I reached into my wallet and extracted one of my joke business cards, which I used only on my trips. Corbett was the only person in Belleville who had been privileged to be handed one, and he kept it pinned up on his refrigerator. Whenever I was on vacation, I had the strange habit of sticking one of the little cards inside the Gideon Bibles in most of my hotel rooms. I had been marking my rooms in this way for several years ever since I had the little devils prepared.

I handed one of the cards to Father Tim.

It was quite colorful and showed a caricature of me with my hand in a little old lady's purse while she gazed off in the distance. A word balloon came out of my mouth spouting the slogan "I NEVER MET A WIDOW I COULDN'T SWINDLE". At the bottom of the card was my name, office address and phone number.

"Maybe you can refer some rich Texas women to me," I quipped. "I'm perfectly willing to cheat American widows too. I pride myself on not discriminating against anyone with money."

Before Timothy could even reply, the clerk at the airline counter announced that we could begin pre-boarding in a few minutes. The priest immediately excused himself while he hurried over to a nearby washroom.

CHAPTER 5 (That's the Kind of Guy I Am)

While Father Timothy was heading off to the bathroom, a large black fellow rushed toward the ticket counter and my attention was diverted to him.

"Traffic was a bitch," he moaned to the clerk. "I didn't think I was going to make it here on time."

The female employee examined the man's ticket and told him that the flight had been oversold and unfortunately all the seats had already been assigned. My ears perked up, sensing a potential opportunity.

The guy lost his temper and began ranting at the poor clerk.

"This is pure bullshit! I purchased this ticket on-line last week. If the damn plane was already full, tell me why they still sold me the ticket."

The flustered attendant stammered, "Please be patient for a moment sir, while I try to reach my supervisor."

She then called someone but I couldn't overhear what she was saying softly into the telephone. She calmly picked up the microphone and announced that the flight was oversold by one ticket and asked if anyone would be willing to take a later flight.

That was my cue and I stood up and sauntered over to the counter.

"I might be interested in changing my travel plans. When is the next flight and what sort of compensation are you offering?"

The woman checked her screen for a moment and then paused to announce that pre-boarding could commence for anyone requiring additional time or travelling with small children.

That task completed, she turned to me and replied, "The next available flight is tomorrow morning at ten o'clock. We can offer you a hotel room for tonight including shuttle fares, a meal voucher for $25 and $75 in cash compensation."

I paused briefly as if I was seriously considering that paltry offer.

"I guess not, then. That's not worth it to me. I'd still get charged for my hotel room tonight in Las Vegas."

I looked up at the huge dude.

"Sorry, big guy; hopefully someone else will come forward."

I turned to walk back to my seat.

"Wait man, I'm desperate here. I've got plans to meet friends later tonight. How much will it take to let me have your seat?"

I evaluated the gentleman and spotted a designer watch. His clothes and carry-on bag were clearly top of the line and two fingers on each of his hands sported gaudy gold and diamond rings. This guy exuded money and my overall impression was that he must be some type of drug dealer.

"I guess I could be persuaded for $400 plus what the airline is offering."

"Screw you," the fellow barked. "Do I look like an idiot?"

There was no way I was going to take abuse from this cretin. His outburst was entirely uncalled for.

"Don't make me answer that," I replied sarcastically. "By the way, my price just went up to five hundred bucks. Take it or leave it. You've got thirty seconds to decide."

"Come on man, have a heart. You're trying to rob me."

"I'm a lawyer. That's what we do. Besides, from the look of that Rolex and those rings, you're not hurting for money."

The man broke out laughing and said, "It's a deal."

He peeled off five Bennies from his wallet and handed them to me.

The clerk cancelled my boarding pass and issued a replacement to the black guy who, by the way, never thanked me for giving up my seat.

I walked back to sit with Father Timothy.

"I won't be joining you on the flight after all, Tim. The flight was oversold and that big gentleman was desperate to get on the plane so I transferred my ticket to him. I'll be arriving in Las Vegas late tomorrow morning. Tell you what, since my room tonight at the Las Vegas Club is already paid for and non-refundable, here's my E-mail payment receipt. I'll phone the hotel shortly and advise them that you'll be the one checking in to the room. At least that way you'll have a bed for tonight and tomorrow you can contact the church."

"That's so kind of you, Boyd. I really appreciate this."

"It's my pleasure. Look, when you land at the Las Vegas airport, just follow the crowd off the plane and go to the ground transportation area. It's well marked. You can get a shuttle bus ticket at one of the kiosks for about eight bucks and it'll take you right downtown to the Las Vegas Club. They're calling your row number now. Have a great flight and I'd love to treat you to some meals while you're in Las Vegas. You can find me at the El Cortez."

"Thank you so much, Boyd. It's been fascinating speaking with you. By the way, that was extremely generous giving up your ticket like that to help out a stranger."

"That's the kind of guy I am, Tim. Make sure you look me up and I'll show you around my favorite city."

The priest joined the line to board the plane and waved to me just before he walked down the jet-way.

About ten minutes later the clerk beckoned me over to the counter and handed me the $75 in cash, the $25 meal voucher, a confirmation form for my room tonight and two shuttle passes to get to and from the hotel. She was also able to issue my boarding pass for tomorrow morning's flight.

I was exceedingly pleased with myself. Ripping off that drug pusher for $500 was even more fun than fleecing a trusting old widow.

When I got to the hotel I used a phone card that I had purchased on my last trip to Vegas and called the Las Vegas Club.

The desk clerk tried to give me a hard time, insisting that my room wasn't transferable, but I held my ground. I was both overbearing and rude, and threatened to speak directly with the manager, pointing out that I was a very regular customer there and that I was already booked for six nights at their sister hotel, the Plaza.

That sealed the deal and the clerk assured me that he had now added Father Timothy Camacho onto the computer records so there would be no difficulty when the priest arrived to check in.

For my free supper I had the Montreal smoked meat sandwich with fries, which was only $9.99, and I used up the rest of the $25 meal voucher for three beer and the tip.

A free continental breakfast was also included with my hotel room.

My mood bordered on ecstatic all evening as I wallowed contentedly in my freebies and savored life in general.

This had been the most lucrative airline overbooking bonanza I had ever scored.

## CHAPTER 6 (A Priest in Las Vegas)

Father Timothy found his assigned seat on the plane and placed his carry-on bag in the overhead bin. He apologized as he disturbed the large African-American gentleman in the aisle seat in order to get situated in his own window seat.

Tim was somewhat apprehensive about what lay ahead, never having flown before.

He smiled at his seating companion and gushed, "That was very kind of Mr. Billingsworth to give up his seat for you."

"Do you actually know that shyster?"

"I just met him today. He's remarkably generous for a lawyer."

"You've got to be kidding. He extorted $500 out of me in addition to the money and hotel room the airline gave him. He's a greedy scumbag."

"Oh dear, I wasn't aware of that. He indicated that he stayed behind out of the goodness of his heart."

"Has any lawyer ever told the truth about anything? The only thing he was kind to was his own wallet. I feel like my pocket's been picked but I really needed to get to Las Vegas this evening. The creep knew he had me over a barrel. I hope his damn plane crashes tomorrow."

Timothy didn't know how to respond to such a vicious comment so he kept quiet.

It was quite frightening as the huge plane hurtled down the runway and lifted off. How was it possible for such a heavy object to stay up in the air? Timothy silently prayed to God for protection.

After about ten minutes the fear subsided and was replaced with exhilaration. Timothy was actually flying.

The big passenger, who introduced himself as Leroy, was most talkative and Timothy listened in fascination to tales of gang wars and life growing up in a tough section of Houston.

Leroy never disclosed how he made his money, but over the course of the flight admitted that he earned over half a million dollars a year and paid no taxes.

Timothy silently puzzled over the massive earnings made by the two men he had spoken to so far on this vacation. They made more money in a couple of weeks than Timothy garnered over the course of an entire year.

Leroy hadn't even finished high school. There was something unsettling, possibly even highly unjust, in this obscene income disparity.

It was night as they approached Las Vegas and Timothy gasped in wonderment when the blazing lights of the city came into view.

Leroy was most anxious to get off the airplane and managed to bully his way almost to the front of the plane by the time the door opened to permit passengers to exit.

Timothy remained in his seat until it was his turn to leave. As Boyd had instructed, Tim followed the crowd onto a tram and then down an escalator where he spotted the "GROUND TRANSPORTATION" sign.

He asked a man where the shuttle bus kiosks were located and purchased a ticket with CLS. The vendor told Tim to take a seat in the bus directly across the street.

Timothy kept his small carry-on bag on his lap as he was too fearful of allowing the

driver to stow the bag in the rear baggage
compartment in case his belongings were
stolen.

He had been warned by parishioners not to
travel with a suitcase since checked baggage
was costly and often misplaced.

After a few minutes the shuttle filled up
and the driver got in and pulled away.

The neon lights were fantastic and Timothy
was thrilled with the free tour as the small
bus made at least half a dozen stops on the
Strip before eventually heading downtown.

When the driver announced the Las Vegas
Club, Timothy stepped off the bus and entered
the hotel.

The small line-up at the check-in counter
moved along quickly and there was no
difficulty in obtaining Boyd's room. Timothy
was a bit embarrassed when he disclosed to the
clerk that he didn't own a personal credit
card. The diocese provided a credit card but
it could only be used for church business so
Tim had left it back in his tiny apartment.

Timothy declined to pay a cash deposit in
order to activate the room telephone, deciding
that he didn't need a phone and fearful that
perhaps the money wouldn't be returned to him
in the morning.

He found the elevators and was soon
unlocking the door to Room 924.

Tim was very pleased with the room which
looked out over another hotel across the
street. He had a great view of the rooftop
swimming pool there.

The priest got down on his knees and
thanked God for delivering him safe and sound
to Las Vegas and for introducing him to such
interesting fellow travelers.

Then he counted his money. His total holiday net worth was now only $192 and Timothy asked God to help him survive the entire week on such limited funds.

Too timid even to venture back downstairs let alone go outside at night, Father Tim again expressed his humble thanks to God for providing this free hotel room through the hands of a complete stranger.

On Sunday morning Timothy awoke refreshed and optimistic. He had been so thoroughly exhausted the night before. Travelling was most tiring.

He threw open the drapes and looked out on a beautiful sunny day. His heart soared with anticipation. He truly had made it to exotic Las Vegas.

Timothy showered and donned his clerical garb. The huge telephone book in the drawer contained a city map and Father Tim tried to locate the Catholic churches. Only one was anywhere near the downtown area but Tim felt too apprehensive to attempt to walk there. He jotted down the telephone number and went down to the hotel lobby to find a pay phone.

Since it was Sunday, Timothy was hopeful that someone would answer the church phone.

As luck would have it, Timothy actually reached one of the priests.

"Good morning, Father. My name is Father Tim Camacho from east Texas. I find myself here in Las Vegas with slightly insufficient funds and I'm hoping that the church can put me up in its living quarters for a few nights to enable my money to stretch."

The response was most disheartening.

"I'm so sorry Father Tim, but you couldn't have picked a worse week. There's a retreat on in town for several of the convents in this part of the country, and all of our parochial houses are fully occupied by the sisters. We've even had to stuff four or more bodies into each room, so we simply can't accommodate you right now. If you wish, I could request our administrative assistant to call around on your behalf tomorrow when the church office opens. Perhaps she could locate an inexpensive motel for you."

"Thank you so much for the offer, but that won't be necessary. I'll just make do with the money I brought and I'm sure that God will provide for me."

Father Tim was starving. He walked outside in search of a place to have breakfast. Once he had food in his stomach, Timothy believed that he would be able to better assess his predicament.

He hadn't walked fifty feet when a scruffy young man approached him.

"Excuse me, Father. I haven't eaten in two days. Can you possibly spare a bit of change?"

"Oh, that's dreadful; of course I can help you, son."

Timothy took a five dollar bill out of his wallet and handed it to the filthy young fellow who thanked him profusely and walked off.

There was a donut shop in the next hotel so Timothy ate a sandwich and coffee there. That revived him and he decided to return to his hotel room and figure out how he was going to find someplace to sleep for the next few nights. Check-out wasn't until noon.

Again, on the very short walk back to the Las Vegas Club, another man perhaps in his forties accosted Timothy.

"Hey, friend, can you spare three bucks for bus fare? I've got to get clear across to the other side of the city and I'm flat broke."

Timothy fished out three one dollar bills and handed them to the man, suddenly becoming anxious himself that his own paltry trip money was quickly depleting.

Was God putting Timothy through some sort of test?

All these needy people were emerging out of the woodwork. There were no panhandlers back home in Timothy's tiny rural parish.

## CHAPTER 7 (A Message from God)

Back in Room 924, Timothy packed his bag and pondered what to do.

As he checked all the drawers to ensure that he had left nothing behind, Tim discovered a Gideon Bible and decided to let God surprise him with this morning's bible reading.

Instead of using his own Catholic bible, Timothy picked up the Gideon Bible and prayed to God to provide some guidance to his financial predicament.

Tim flipped open the bible randomly and looked down. The good book had opened at Psalm 85 and some sort of small card was wedged into that page.

Tim picked up the card and saw a smiling caricature looking back at him. It looked vaguely familiar.

A closer inspection revealed that the man's hand was surreptitiously placed in a grey-haired woman's handbag and the man was saying something rude about swindling widows.

Timothy's eyes dropped down to the bottom of the card and he gasped in bewilderment.

It was the business card of Boyd Billingsworth, the Canadian lawyer Timothy had just met yesterday.

His hands trembling, Tim fumbled around in his wallet and extracted an identical card.

This was an impossible coincidence.

God's message was loud and clear.

Timothy could seek help from his new lawyer friend.

Tim read Psalm 85 but without clear illumination about how it related to his predicament. It was a plea to God to finally forgive His people and lead them out of their desperate plight. The psalm expressed a faithful hope for peace and prosperity.

Father Tim checked out of the Las Vegas Club and asked for directions to the El Cortez Hotel.

It was set apart from the rest of the downtown casinos and Timothy walked there and waited in the check-in area at the El Cortez. He would submit this new accommodation dilemma to Boyd Billingsworth and trust that God's message was sending Tim to the right place.

Timothy mulled over the situation.

Was it really likely that a heartless attorney who bragged about cheating elderly ladies would take pity on an impecunious old priest?

Timothy severely doubted it but was reminded of the parable of the Good Samaritan. Help had come from the unlikeliest of sources to rescue that stranded and desperate traveler.

...

Meanwhile, my wake-up call came as requested at seven o'clock and I devoured my free continental breakfast in the hotel lobby before catching the shuttle bus back to the Houston airport.

This flight was close to an hour late departing so it was almost one o'clock when I finally entered the El Cortez.

As I approached the check-in counter, a voice called out my name.

I turned in the direction of the greeting and saw Father Tim sitting on a small couch. I walked over and shook his hand.

"Great to see you again, Father. Did everything go smoothly at the Las Vegas Club?"

"Yes, it was lovely. Thank you again for your generosity. Please accept my deepest apologies for stalking you, but another dilemma has sprung up and I thought I'd seek your counsel since you're so familiar with Las Vegas."

I sat down beside the priest, amused at this turn of events and curious as to what problem had surfaced so quickly. Timothy was certainly a fish out of water in Las Vegas.

"What trouble could you possibly have gotten yourself into in such a short time?" I teased.

"My expectation of a free room didn't materialize through my church. They were already stuffed to the rafters hosting a retreat for nuns. I'm hoping that your knowledge of this city will enable you to direct me to where I can find affordable accommodation."

"Sure, I should be able to find you a cheap room. How much money have you got left?"

"So far the only money I've spent has been for the shuttle bus, a modest breakfast and a couple of sad panhandlers who approached me for assistance. I still have $180 but I need to keep back $10 to cover the shuttle bus back to the airport."

I pulled a tiny calculator out of my bag and tapped away. The results were discouraging.

"Even if you managed to eat on ten bucks a day and spent nothing else, that would still only leave you with less than $20 a night for a room. A few years ago it was possible to get a cheap room downtown, but not these days. I'm afraid that you're screwed, Timothy. You'll just have to trust your God to keep dropping money in your path. Good luck."

I stood up and joined the check-in line. What kind of simpleton comes to Vegas with empty pockets? Surely the priest didn't expect me to finance his vacation.

A couple of minutes later I glanced over at the sofa where Tim had been lurking in wait for me, and I was pleased to see that he was gone.

I was in town to enjoy myself, not to rescue fools.

My turn came and I stepped up to the available check-in clerk and handed her my Expedia internet receipt.

"I've requested Room 321 in the old section of the hotel. Is it available for me?"

The clerk confirmed that my favorite room had indeed been reserved for me. While she was doing the paperwork and preparing my room keys, I heard a familiar voice off to my right. I looked over and saw the priest at the adjoining wicket. Curious, I decided to eavesdrop.

The clerk was saying, "I'm so sorry sir, but this hotel is fully booked all week, and our understanding is that all the downtown hotels are also fully occupied. There are two major slot tournaments going on. Normally we can refer clients to other establishments when we're full up, but unfortunately you've arrived without a room at the worst possible time."

The forlorn expression on the priest's face was pitiful. He looked like a terrified deer caught in the headlights of an oncoming truck.

I decided to intervene after all.

"Father Tim, come over here," I ordered.

He complied.

I turned to the lady looking after me.

"My priestly friend here has no place to stay. He foolishly arrived without pre-booking a hotel. Can I change my Room 321 to another room with two beds?"

The clerk checked her computer screen and after a few moments of searching, answered in the negative.

"Since I'm not a young altar boy, I guess I don't really have to fear spending a few nights in the same room with the priest," I joked, "but I certainly don't want to sleep in the same bed with him. Can I arrange to have one of your portable cots brought up to my room?"

Father Tim remained totally silent. I glanced down at him and realized that his eyes were closed and he was praying.

A moment later the lady confirmed that there was an available cot and that it would be delivered to the room immediately.

The clerk handed me a folder containing two room keys.

"Do you require directions to find the room?" she inquired.

"No, I've stayed in this room many times before. I really appreciate your assistance with the cot. Will there be any additional charges?"

"No sir, the room rate is the same whether one or two guests occupy the room, and the portable cot is complimentary. Please enjoy your stay with us."

I turned to the priest.

"Okay, Father Tim, follow me. We're going to be roommates for the next six nights. I hope you don't fart in your sleep."

"How would I know? Look, Boyd, I really didn't intend to impose on your privacy. Won't your holiday be ruined having me hovering around?"

"Nonsense! I'll have to cancel the hookers but other than that, I'm sure we'll get along just fine. We're both well-educated and about the same age. As an added bonus, I've got a ton of two-for-one coupons. Feeding you won't cost me a penny."

We had reached the small stairway which led up to the third floor which was the top level of the old section of the El Cortez.

"This portion of the hotel was built in 1941 and the rooms are quite spacious. We won't get in each other's way at all. Stop worrying about everything. We're both on vacation and we're in Vegas to enjoy ourselves."

I unlocked the door to Room 321 and pushed it open.

The reason I always requested this room was because of the great layout.

We walked down a small hallway. The bathroom was to the left. At the end of the hallway, a large and lovely room was spread out before us.

To the left was a sofa and coffee table. In the center section of the room there was a soft armchair facing a dresser on top of which was perched a TV.

At the far end of the room there was a king size bed and two night tables.

"This is a very opulent room," the priest gushed. "Thank you so much for sharing it with me."

Just then there was a knock on the door and housekeeping wheeled in a portable cot and showed us how to open it up. She left the spare bedding and I tipped her and told her that we'd make up the cot ourselves once we had decided where to place it.

"This cot takes up more space than I expected," I announced to Timothy. "I'm not sure where the best place is to set it up. Do you have any preference as to where you sleep?"

"No, Boyd, I'll just leave it up to you."

"I've just had a thought. There's another small room behind this door. I wonder if the cot can fit in there. If it does, then we'll both have a lot more privacy."

I opened the door. The extra room was quite tiny and contained a small writing desk and chair. I got Tim to help me drag the desk out into the main room, and then we wheeled the cot into the little room. It was a bit snug once we opened it up, but it still gave Timothy enough space to get out of bed and close the door. The little room even had its own tiny closet so he could hang up his clothes there.

It only took us a few minutes to unpack our belongings since we had each brought just one small sports bag as a carry-on.

"For a novice traveler, you at least had the good sense not to lug a suitcase along with you. I'm also impressed that you were astute enough to contact me when your church rejected you. I guess the nine years you spent in university was worthwhile after all. What made you think to come looking for me?"

"Actually God provided the inspiration in a most unique way. He sent me a direct message to contact you."

I must have had a puzzled expression on my face because the priest elaborated.

"God led me to your business card which I found in a bible in my hotel room at the Las

Vegas Club. His sign couldn't have been any clearer that you were the vessel through which he was pouring out the assistance I so badly needed."

"I think your memory is failing, Timothy. I gave you my joke business card in the Houston airport."

"That's true enough, and I still have that one, but now I have two of them."

Timothy opened his wallet and triumphantly displayed two identical cards.

"See," he exclaimed, "God duplicated your card and placed it where He knew I'd find it."

"I despair over your naïve gullibility, Father Tim. Go check and see if there's a Gideon Bible in this room."

The priest looked perplexed but opened the drawers to the small bedside tables and discovered this room's bible.

"Now open it to the Psalms section and see if anything strange pops out."

Timothy did so, riffled through the pages and out fell a small card. He picked it up, glanced at it and let out a gasp.

With a most dumbfounded look, he mumbled, "I don't understand. It's another one of your revolting cards. What's happening?"

"Sorry to burst your bubble of faith, Timothy, but God didn't plant those cards. I did. I don't have the nerve to show them around my hometown, but whenever I'm on vacation, I place one in the Gideon Bible in each hotel room I occupy. I visit Las Vegas several times a year and tend to specifically request the same room I've had previously if I liked it. You must have been given Room 924 in the Las Vegas Club. I stayed there a couple of times last year and liked the layout so I asked for it again this time around. It's the same with this Room 321. Your finding my card was just coincidence, not divine intervention."

Timothy was speechless as he tried to digest my explanation of his so-called miracle.

As my little gratuitous dig at religion, I added, "The fact that my cards are still in all these bibles is pretty conclusive proof that nobody ever bothers to read them. People in Vegas pray to Lady Luck, not to God."

CHAPTER 8 (Polar Opposites)

Since we each had a room key, Timothy insisted on giving me some privacy and he left to take a walk around the area.

We agreed to meet back in the room at six o'clock in order to grab some supper together.

I sat on the couch to unwind for a while. Travel became increasingly tiring as I relentlessly got older. This particular stint had involved a full day and a half in various airports.

Despite Jim Corbett's mockery of my travel bonanzas, I was still thrilled with the marvelous coup I had pulled off by scoring over $575 in cash compensation plus the meal and hotel in Houston.

It had been well worth the extra travel time and had significantly driven down the eventual total cost of this vacation.

My next chore was to head out for beer and I purchased a twelve-pack of American beer and some cheap snacks to eat in the room.

I sorted through the various meal and tour coupons I had accumulated in the mail since my last jaunt to Las Vegas in December.

Having no family, I found it pleasant to visit Las Vegas each Christmas. Playing slots and watching the crowds eradicated any loneliness that I would have felt had I stayed in Belleville alone at that most vulnerable time of year for single men.

Finally I went downstairs to the casino and played Caveman Keno slots for three hours. I lost twenty bucks but enjoyed myself. It was good to be back in town.

Timothy was already in the room by the time I returned and I asked how he had managed to amuse himself all afternoon.

"I walked all around just taking in the sights and I chatted with several residents who approached me for a bit of financial assistance. Did you realize that there's a lot of poverty hidden behind these ostentatious monuments to opulence and excess?"

"Did you realize that those bums are mostly drunks and drug addicts? They'll say anything to persuade you to part with some money. I remember one young woman who used to toss out the line, 'Can you spare something so I can feed my baby?' Even I fell for that gimmick once or twice until I noticed her trip after trip pulling the same stunt. You're wasting what little money you have by falling for those fake sob stories."

"I firmly disagree. It's both wiser and kinder to give these unfortunates the benefit of the doubt. I'll not harden my heart by judging them. That's against my Catholic beliefs. Besides, it's always possible that the person asking for your help is really Jesus himself testing your morals."

I looked over at the priest in disgust but held my tongue.

Finally I just said, "Suit yourself. There's some cold beer on ice in the wastebasket. Would you like one?"

"Yes, thank you, Boyd. I'm quite hot and tired from my long walk."

I grabbed a can of beer for each of us and asked Timothy what kind of food he felt like for supper.

"Anything will be acceptable," he replied. "I'll let you choose. If you prefer to dine in an expensive restaurant, please do so, and I'll find a place I can afford."

"Don't worry. I avoid the rip-off joints. There's no way I'll blow $29.95 on a steak dinner. I've been checking over my discount vouchers and I found a whole bunch of two-for-one deals. I've decided to call them my 'PRIESTS EAT FREE' coupons."

"Boyd, please don't feel that you have to entertain me or spend excessive time with me. I'm extremely grateful that you're willing to share your hotel room with me."

"Tim, you're not a nuisance or a burden of any sort, so stop worrying about everything. I can honestly say that I'm pleased to have a roommate to talk with on this trip, especially someone like you who looks at everything through innocent, kindly eyes. We might even learn something from each other."

"That's a very nice thing to say. I have been fretting about ruining your vacation. Is there anything I can do to be less disruptive?"

"There's one minor matter, but what you do about it is entirely up to you."

"Certainly, just name it."

"Do you have to wear your monkey suit everywhere? I don't think gamblers like to see a priest in their casino. You're probably making everyone uncomfortable."

Timothy started to laugh and then composed himself.

"Of course, Boyd; removing my priestly garb is a simple concession to your generosity. The trouble is that I didn't bring any ordinary clothes with me. How do you suggest we make me blend in around here?"

"I brought plenty of clothes. My pants are too long to fit you but there's nothing wrong with your pants. It's just the upper half of your wardrobe that upsets people."

I went to the dresser and began opening the drawers, extracting one of my casino jerseys and a grey sweatshirt, both items bearing casino logos.

"Here; try these on. You may as well be a walking billboard for the casinos."

Timothy took the garments into his little room and emerged a minute later wearing my duds.

"Perfect; now you look like you belong in Las Vegas and I won't feel like a fraud giving people the false impression that I must be some kind of saint because I'm hanging out with a priest."

While we drank a second brew, Timothy told me in more detail where he had walked today.

"Didn't you walk through any of the casinos?" I asked.

"This was the only one I had to enter in order to get up to our room. It didn't seem appropriate to be in a casino on a Sunday. I believe I'd prefer to stay in this hotel this evening if you don't mind. I'm quite weary. Please don't let me cramp your style, though. I don't need a babysitter."

"Look, I've got almost two full weeks in Vegas so I'm fine with staying in the El Cortez tonight. Are you hungry yet?"

"I could eat now but I'm not ravenous."

"Does the church permit you to watch people on a Sunday?"

"Of course."

"Can you drink alcohol on a Sunday while watching people?"

"I'm drinking alcohol right now and watching you, am I not?"

"What if some of the people you're watching are gambling in the casino while you're watching them?"

"I'm sure that would be acceptable to God so long as I'm not gambling."

"Great! In that case let me treat you to an evening of education learning what makes gamblers tick. We can sit downstairs in a bar overlooking the casino and even eat there when we get hungry. You'll learn a lot more being dressed like everyone else. People aren't themselves around a priest. They're always on their best behavior. That's probably why you have the warped view that people are basically honest and considerate."

"Most people are that way," Timothy countered. "It's you who has the distorted view about folks."

## CHAPTER 9 (A Vegas Education)

We finished our beer and wandered downstairs just after seven o'clock to a piano bar overlooking the main casino floor.

I insisted that we sit at a small table in the corner by the railing so we could see and hear a good deal of the action.

We each ordered a beer using one of my two-for-one coupons. I had a whole raft of them but unfortunately only one per day was permitted for drinks.

There was a small poker room directly behind us and a row of slot machines just eight feet away. You couldn't get any closer to gambling and I sensed that Timothy was a bit uncomfortable.

"Are we pushing the envelope of your Catholic faith by being here?"

"I'm not entirely sure," he responded. "It's certainly busy and noisy."

"A casino is an exciting place, especially at night once the patrons get all liquored up. Drinks are free while you gamble."

"That's disgusting," Timothy blurted out. "What an abhorrent combination, gambling and alcohol!"

"The casino industry prefers to call it 'gaming' which sounds more civilized. The cocktail waitresses can make a fantastic income. Try to keep tabs on this pretty little number in the skimpy outfit. She's taking drink orders right now as she's making her rounds, and she'll follow the same route all evening, just like a mailman. It's exactly twenty minutes past seven. When she walks by in a few minutes, try to count the number of drinks on her tray."

59

Four and a half minutes later the waitress strolled right by us again.

"She's carrying at least twenty drinks," Timothy informed me.

Six minutes later she returned with a tray of empties, and in another five minutes she was striding past us again with fresh drinks.

"Since it's early in the evening, the average tip is only about a dollar, and she'll take a ten minute break every hour, which means she can complete three round trips every hour. Right now she's making about $60 an hour. By midnight most of the male patrons will be loaded and salivating over her hot little body, so her average tip will skyrocket and she'll rake in almost $200 every hour. Hers is one of the best jobs in Vegas. The girls at the big Strip casinos make much more because their customers are wealthier. There's big money for some of the little people when liquor and gambling are combined."

"She must be exhausted by the end of her shift," Timothy commented.

"The cocktail girls do work mighty hard, but in Las Vegas you've got to hustle to be successful. Those panhandlers you insist on throwing your money at don't want to work at all."

"I find that hard to believe, Boyd. The ones I spoke with were lamenting that they run into one roadblock after another with the employment system here."

"Most of them are just spinning you a line. They make more money begging than anyone working in fast food or any other low level job around here. That's why you'll see the same faces panhandling year after year. It's their job and they'll say anything to get you to cough up some dough. It's naïve do-gooders like you who keep them pestering tourists on the street and wasting their lives away."

"I'll take your rather jaded point of view under advisement," was Timothy's only response.

We ordered another beer.

A man got off his stool at one of the nearby slot machines and left with a disgusted look on his face.

"It doesn't appear as if that gentleman had much fun," Timothy remarked.

A minute later a lady sat down at the same machine.

"Let's keep tabs on this woman," I suggested. "She's just about to put some money into her slot machine."

Her credit meter immediately showed 5,000 credits.

"She's just inserted a fifty dollar bill into the machine," I told Tim. "It's a penny denomination slot game she's playing."

"Why would she put so much money in at once if it only takes a penny to play it?"

"They're called penny machines but there's a catch. This particular type of machine is called Reels O'Dublin. I've played them myself and they're a lot of fun, but in order to qualify for all the special features, you have to place a bet on all the lines plus make an extra bet to trigger the bonus features. When I played them I only bet one cent per line but I still had to bet thirty cents minimum in order to get access to the bonus features. The maximum bet is three bucks. Let's see how much this lady likes to wager."

The woman hit the "MAXIMUM BET" button and her credit meter dropped to 4,700.

"She's playing the limit. It won't take her long to burn through fifty bucks unless she gets lucky quickly."

The machine spun and then bells went off and lights flashed with the word "WIN" prominently displayed.

"She is lucky," Timothy observed. "How much did she win?"

"She won fifty credits on one line, so actually she lost $2.50 on that particular spin."

"But the machine told her she was a winner," Timothy persisted.

"She was, but only on one of the twenty possible lines. That's one of the gimmicks of this brand of slot. It gives you lots of tiny jackpots accompanied by bells and whistles, but in reality your credit meter keeps dropping lower. The only way to do well is to hit something decent when you're in the bonus mode. Eventually she'll get there and I'll explain it to you more fully."

Less than ten minutes later the woman was out of credits, but she dug into her purse and slipped another fifty dollar bill into the machine. That money only lasted her fifteen minutes but she was persistent and fed yet another fifty into the slot.

"That poor woman has lost $100 already and she's putting in more money," Timothy lamented. "I don't understand the attraction at all."

"Be patient. If she hits something you'll see first-hand why people are addicted to the thrill of the slots."

We each ordered another beer plus a hot dog with potato chips when the piano bar waitress came around to our table. I was already feeling no pain from the beer I'd

already consumed, but I was thoroughly
enjoying myself.

Finally the lady hit two bonus symbols.
The machine made a strange sound as the two
reels with the symbols remained stationary
while the remaining three reels continued to
spin. One by one those reels stopped to reveal
that she had not hit the third bonus symbol
which was required to get into the bonus
round. The woman groaned.

Five minutes later she was out of credits
again but doggedly inserted another fifty into
the slot machine.

Just then the machine beside her became
vacant and a friend of the woman sat down and
began playing. We could hear their
conversation clearly despite the casino noise.

"Have you hit anything yet, Molly?"

"I've been close but nothing big so far."

"How much have you lost?"

"Just fifty bucks."

"That woman lied to her friend," Timothy
whispered. "She's lost $150 already."

"Gamblers don't like to admit their
losses. They just focus on the joy of playing
and the jackpots they do manage to hit."

Soon the telltale sound of another
potential bonus round filled the air around
us. Both Timothy and I watched in anticipation
as the reels slowed down and stopped. This
time the third symbol did appear in the right
spot and the woman shrieked with delight.

"Now the bonus round begins," I explained.
"She's won fifteen free spins and any jackpot
she hits pays out eight times the normal
amount. This is her best opportunity to make
some real money."

Watching the free spins was quite
mesmerizing and from time to time the woman

hit something. The machine would then stop temporarily each time to permit the credit meter to add the new win to the existing jackpot.

When she was almost out of free spins, two of the three symbols showed up again and the eerie noise of the bonus feature kicked in. The third symbol did in fact show up and both the woman and her friend screamed in unison.

"She's won an additional eight free spins," I explained to Timothy.

Again an occasional jackpot was won on those free spins and when they were finally used up, the machine flashed the words "BIG WIN" as it announced the final bonus jackpot of 10,250 credits.

"My word," Timothy raved, "she's won more than $10,000."

"Not quite," I grinned. "The lady won 10,250 pennies which works out to $102.50. Look how excited she is right now. Keep watching her and you may discover why casinos are so successful."

For a few minutes the woman just stared happily at her slot screen while she finished her drink and waited for another to arrive. Her friend got back to playing her own machine since the excitement had now subsided.

Over the ensuing hour Tim and I ate our food and had two more beer each while the woman gradually lost all her credits and then another $50.

As she stood up to leave, the woman's husband showed up and we overheard her gushing to him.

"Honey, I won $102.50. What a fantastic machine! I've never had so much fun. How did you do at the blackjack table?"

We couldn't hear his response since they were walking away from us.

"That lady lied again," Timothy blurted out. "She lost $250 while we've been watching her but she's acting like she won. Can you explain that?"

"Casino magic" was my only reply.

By now it was almost midnight.

I was a bit unsteady as we made our way back to our room. My head was spinning but the priest didn't appear the least bit intoxicated.

## CHAPTER 10 (Vegas the Magnificent)

I felt like crap the next morning when I finally woke up with a massive hangover.

Even though it was watered-down American beer, I must have polished off seven including the two in the room before we went downstairs.

I sat up.

The priest was sitting cheerfully on the sofa, already dressed and reading an entertainment magazine supplied free by the hotel. I was pleased to note that he was wearing my casino shirt and not his priest's paraphernalia.

"I've got a splitting headache," I moaned. "How do you feel?"

"I feel great. I've had my shower and feel ready to conquer the world. For some fortunate reason I never experience hangovers no matter how much alcohol I've consumed."

"That must be God's little gift to his flock of alkies," I snarled.

"Now, now Boyd, there's no reason to get blasphemous. You indicated last evening that we'd venture over to the Strip today. When would you like to get started?"

"We can leave right after we've had breakfast. Look, it's going to be too hot for you wearing those heavy priest pants today. Are you willing to wear a pair of my shorts if they fit?"

"Sure, that would be great."

Luckily our waist size was very similar and my shorts fit Timothy almost perfectly.

We made small talk over breakfast and then caught the Deuce bus south to the Strip. We managed to get a seat at the extreme front of the double-decker bus on the upper level which meant that Timothy could get a magnificent view during the ride.

"Where did you learn to drink like that?" I asked once the bus got moving. "You matched me beer for beer and didn't show any ill effects."

Timothy blushed.

"Being a priest in a small parish is an extremely solitary life. In some ways I'm violating my priestly obligations when I drink to excess, because I'm supposed to be constantly on call in case someone requires my services urgently, but I'm unable to maintain that level of dedication. Alcohol takes some of the sting out of the depressingly lonely periods."

"Don't you have any drinking buddies?"

"No, I'm the only priest in the parish. Larger parishes require additional clergy which means live-in friends with similar outlooks, but I'm totally on my own. It's very difficult for a priest to develop a friendship with anyone other than a fellow priest."

"What are your views on permitting priests to marry?" I queried.

"It really doesn't matter what I think. No one in the church hierarchy is going to listen to the likes of me. You said you've lived on your own for over twenty-five years. Do you drink alone too much?"

"I guess it's all relative. I do drink alone quite often but I've got one really close friend, a retired lawyer I've known for over forty years. I walk over to his condo every Saturday night and we get tanked and yak about anything and everything. He's got a warped sense of humor just like I do, and he can see right through me if I start talking bullshit. Jim is the complete opposite of me.

In fact he's almost your clone, completely kind and gullible, and so far I haven't been able to talk him out of that nonsense."

"Are you really as hardened as you claim?"

"Definitely! Take the panhandlers around here, for instance. You can't say no to any of them. For me it takes the perfect line at the right time before I'll cough up a dime. It's unusual for me to hand out money to a single bum on any of my trips, and I've been like that ever since I was a young man. My late wife was more like you, totally forgiving and compassionate."

By then the bus had reached the Stratosphere so for the remainder of the ride I pointed out the sights of Las Vegas.

We got off the bus at Mandalay Bay which is at the extreme south end of the Strip. For a while we walked around inside the hotel and then took a free tram to the Excalibur and headed outdoors to walk around.

Father Tim was aghast when he examined the little whore cards handed out on every street corner along the Strip.

"What do these mean?" he asked.

"Young girls will come to your hotel to dance for you or, for extra cash, provide you with whatever sordid pleasures your naughty fantasies desire."

Timothy thought about that for a moment and then smirked. I asked him what he found so amusing and the first hint of a bawdy sense of humor emerged.

He turned to me and asked with a deadpan expression on his face, "Any idea how much a pair of plump young altar boys might set me back?"

I burst out laughing.

"Bad, bad priest! Now you'll have to say the Hail Mary a thousand times to atone for that distasteful little remark."

"You're right, Boyd, and I'm sorry. It was wrong even to joke about such a repulsive matter."

When we arrived at Caesar's Palace we stood for a short while watching some people play blackjack at a table where the minimum bet was $500. A couple of the men were betting at least $2,000 on each hand.

As we walked away from the table, Timothy vented his disgust at such a flagrant misuse of money, and that prompted a heated discussion.

"It's not your money to spend, Tim. Those fellows earned it and have the right to enjoy it however they please. Besides, there are just too many lazy deadbeats in society these days, sponging off the government and unwilling to do any work. I'd rather see those blackjack players keep the economy humming by coming to Las Vegas than allow the parasites to drink and smoke all of our tax dollars away."

"The whole thrust of the bible is to share," Timothy replied angrily. "What those men lost in a minute could rescue a good family like the one I just spent my life savings on last Friday. The selfishness of the rich appalls me."

"You have no right to spend someone else's money for them," I shot back. "Only the government thinks it has that privilege, and they do a piss-poor job of it. Churches aren't much better. Don't get me started on my opinions about religion."

"You told me in Houston that you attend church every Sunday, sometimes even taking in two services. How can you justify that with your disgust about sharing wealth?"

"I only go to church to drum up new clients to fleece. That's all I'm going to say about the matter right now. Let's put religion on the back burner and enjoy this beautiful day. These casinos represent the very epitome of modern architecture. At least you can appreciate them for that."

"On the contrary, they're nothing but shocking monuments to opulence and perversion, but I'll respect your wishes and keep my opinions to myself so that we can enjoy the remainder of our tour."

Since we had all-day passes for the Deuce buses, we hopped on and off several times so that I could show Timothy around various hotels like the Mirage and the Venetian.

As we walked along a quiet side street near the Fashion Show Mall, I didn't notice that Timothy had stopped at a row of smut racks to gaze in disbelief at the glaring headlines for "YOUNG ASIAN GIRLS" and "BARELY LEGAL" and other catchy come-ons.

A bum was sitting alone on the empty sidewalk.

As I approached him, I noticed his bright orange shirt proclaiming "JESUS LOVES YOU".

"Please spare some change, sir," he asked in a quiet, sad voice.

"Jesus would love you a lot more if you'd get off your deadbeat ass and get a job," I snarled as I walked past the pest in disgust.

That's when I realized that Timothy had fallen behind.

I turned around and watched the priest stop and chat with the beggar. Sure enough, Timothy reached into his wallet and handed some money to the lazy hobo.

I waited while the priest caught up to me.

"That poor man was hungry, Boyd. Surely you didn't ignore him when he asked for help."

"No, I didn't ignore him," I replied truthfully.

"That's good to hear. Perhaps you're growing a heart after all. I'm quite tired now. Are you about ready to head back to our hotel?"

We ate supper back downtown at Magnolia's in the Four Queens. I ordered a large pitcher of Old Town Brown dark beer. We were both so thirsty that it was almost empty by the time our pizzas arrived, so I asked the waitress to bring us a refill.

Timothy was a much faster drinker and as he poured the last drops of the second pitcher into his mug, I remarked caustically, "Your lofty views on sharing sure don't apply to beer. Three days in Las Vegas have already turned you into the very type of selfish human being you pretend to despise."

"He who drinks slowly drinks less," Timothy retorted with a grin. "I think that's in Corinthians."

"At least your timing is perfect. The ten o'clock light show will begin in a few minutes. I think you'll really enjoy it."

Timothy was fascinated with the Fremont Street Experience light show.

Afterwards we wandered around listening to free bands and watching the huge crowds until it was time for the eleven o'clock show. A different light and sound spectacular dazzles the audience each hour after dark until at least midnight.

As we walked through the El Cortez casino on the way to our room, two men got into a shouting match over a slot machine right in front of us and we had to stop.

"That's my machine," the shorter man bellowed. "I just left it for a minute to throw a piss."

"Tough shit, it's mine now," the other fellow retorted.

"Like Hell it is! My player's card is still in the bloody machine."

"Fine, you can have your card back, but there aren't any credits on the machine so you've lost your right to use it. Now bugger off!"

That remark triggered a shoving match.

Two security guards quickly arrived to break up the scuffle. They listened briefly to each man's version of events and then escorted both men out of the casino via separate exits.

Timothy appeared shaken after having witnessed the confrontation.

CHAPTER 11 (Time Share Shenanigans)

On Tuesday morning we both awoke with major hangovers.

"Ha," I joked when Timothy admitted that he had a nasty headache. "God must have abandoned you already. Even He couldn't stomach watching your growing debauchery in Vegas."

"Watching those grown men acting like drunken teenagers last night was extremely upsetting. I know you're simply making fun, but this whole city really makes me wonder if God has given up here. Each time I've entered a casino after dark, I've had the disquieting notion that God wasn't present. You can't begin to imagine how disturbing it is for a priest to feel that way."

"Perhaps you need a change of pace today, Tim. May I interest you in joining me on an excursion to observe the greediest and slimiest operators in Vegas while they ply their vile trade?"

"How is doing that supposed to make me feel better about this city?"

"That's a good point, but what I'm proposing doesn't involve gambling or casinos and it might even be illuminating for you. Consider it to be an educational opportunity."

"Well, since you phrase it that way, I guess I'm in. What exactly are you going to show me?"

"You need to see unfettered greed in action. That's all I'm disclosing right now, but in addition to receiving an education, we'll also score some free meals and a show. Since we'll be given a free breakfast, there's no need to eat anything beforehand. We can begin the learning experience as soon as I've showered and dressed."

Fifteen minutes later we walked into one of the largest casinos downtown. As we entered I cautioned Timothy to let me do all the talking.

Just inside the doorway, a man in a blue blazer flashed a broad smile and gushed, "Morning, folks; can I interest you in a free dinner and show this evening?"

"That sounds great," I answered. "This must be our lucky day."

"Indeed it is, sir. Come with me over to the counter and I'll set you up with the tickets. Where are you gentlemen from?"

"I'm from Canada and my friend is from Texas," I replied.

"How do you like Las Vegas so far?"

"It's fantastic. There's so much to see and do."

"How right you are! Now, I have even more good news. All you have to do to receive the free dinner and show is to permit us to provide you with a lovely complimentary tour of the city on this beautiful sunny day. We'll even throw in a free breakfast."

"Sure, we can do that. How long will the tour take?"

"No more than a couple of hours, and you'll love it. All we need are your names, home addresses and the name of the hotel you're staying in."

Timothy stood there mesmerized by the exchange but clueless as to what was actually happening.

Within five minutes we had been duly processed and then whisked through the casino to a parked shuttle bus on which half a dozen other tourists sat waiting for the tour to begin.

"What exactly is happening?" Timothy whispered.

"We're going on a Time Share tour," I responded.

"What's that?"

"The company is going to try to sell us a unit in one of their resorts. In consideration of taking this tour and listening to their spiel, they'll treat us to supper and a show this evening. It won't cost us a cent and you'll be witness to one of the most successful swindles of the gullible on this planet. I just wish I had gotten in on the action thirty years ago. The profits to be made back then were enormous."

Within ten minutes the small bus was full and the driver pulled away. To save valuable sales time, the tour didn't proceed through the busy stop-and-go traffic on Las Vegas Boulevard. Instead we hurtled down the Interstate heading south, exited just past Mandalay Bay and then finally made a right onto a much quieter section of Las Vegas Boulevard.

All along the way the driver had rattled off a non-stop commentary about which hotels we were passing and what a great vacation destination Las Vegas was.

The bus soon arrived at a small strip plaza where we were all led into a large room and asked to find a seat.

Coffee, juice, donuts and muffins were available so Timothy and I helped ourselves to the free breakfast.

A smiling lady brimming with confidence entered the room and for the next hour we watched a video and listened to her as she explained about the different condominium designs we could choose and what the concept of "Time Share" meant.

Once the film ended, everyone was separated into groups of four. Tim and I were paired off with a married couple from Illinois, and a representative named Ivan introduced himself and advised that he would be our personal tour guide today.

He began chatting pleasantly and instructed us to partake of the buffet luncheon which had just been set up to replace the breakfast items.

Tim and I brought some small sandwiches, cold meats and cheese back to our table even though we weren't really hungry.

When Ivan discovered during the course of our luncheon that I was a lawyer and Timothy was a priest, he focused most of his attention on Stan and Sally from Kankakee.

Ivan then drove the four of us past a nearby casino so that we were aware of how handy it was to the condominium we were about to be shown.

The units themselves were lovely indeed and opulently furnished. Ivan kept repeating how expensive the hotel rooms in Las Vegas had become and how those room prices would continue to soar until only the very wealthy could afford to visit Vegas.

We were whisked back to the Time Share office where another salesman, William, gave a short pep talk to our table. He stressed how easy it was to trade our specified unit of time here for another unit anywhere else in the world, since Las Vegas was so highly sought after.

Sally and Stan were quickly getting sucked in. I had been through these hard sells several times in the past so knew exactly what to expect. Timothy appeared to be enjoying the whole experience immensely.

Ivan escorted the four of us into a small private office and began his polished sales pitch to entice us to sign on the dotted line.

The initial price for a two-week time spot was $34,000 and the company could provide easy financing terms with only a tiny down payment.

Ivan was perceptive and quickly concluded that Tim and I were unlikely to buy anything. He led us back to the presentation area, sat us at our previous table, and said that someone would come around shortly to speak with us. He then rushed back to dazzle Stan and Sally.

"It sounds like an excellent idea for someone like you who vacations here so regularly," Timothy said. "Do you think you'll purchase one?"

"Just keep track of the price changes as these buggers take their best shots at us," I answered.

After a while, William arrived and began his push. When I said we weren't interested, he pressed for a reason.

"It's the price," I replied. "That's a lot of dough for two lousy weeks."

"Tell you what I can do, Boyd. If you don't mind a unit on a lower floor with an inferior view, I can drop the price to $22,000. How does that sound?"

"It's still a lot. I run my own law office and can't take two weeks off all at once. I'd just be wasting the second week most of the time."

Timothy looked at me disapprovingly. He knew I was lying since I was here for two weeks on this trip and had mentioned that I often come for that long.

William wasn't done with his sales pitch.

"I've got just the solution, Boyd. For $12,000 you can purchase a single week per year."

"I don't know. I can't always get away at the exact same week each year depending on business. I probably wouldn't be able to swing it some years."

William was beginning to look peeved and there was another couple who had just been deposited back in this room. He excused himself abruptly and said that someone else would come over to see me.

"It's all very confusing," Timothy whispered. "The price has dropped significantly in just a few minutes. I'm not sure that I understand what's going on."

"Be patient, young man. They're not quite done with us yet."

A buzzer blared in the background and soon all the other couples were escorted back into this room.

A jubilant Ivan squired an ecstatic Stan and Sally back to our table.

He winked at them and they stood up.

Ivan then announced, "Folks, give a hand to Sally and Stan from Kankakee, Illinois, the latest lucky couple to join our fantastic time share family."

Everyone clapped and then other reps made similar announcements as they introduced their new purchasers.

All the new buyers were then escorted out to waiting limousines to be whisked back to their respective hotels.

The rest of us watched through the large windows as the limo doors were opened by uniformed drivers.

Then we waited.

Eventually a woman got around to our table after a whispered consultation with William and Ivan.

"Hello, gentlemen, I'm Darlene, the supervisor. William has advised me of your dilemma, Boyd. I've checked our availabilities and discovered a situation which should suit your needs perfectly. We do have one unit available on a bi-yearly basis and the cost is a remarkably low $6,900. That's why they call me 'The Solvinator' around here. I'm a genius at crafting customized solutions."

"I'm sorry, Darlene. I'm not interested. We'd just like to get the free meal and show tickets we were promised and get back to our hotel."

Without a word, an angry Darlene stood up and stormed off to harass another table.

For another forty-five minutes Timothy and I sat around watching the scummy sales crew flit from table to table, arriving with broad smiles and then departing rudely when they couldn't close a sale.

"See how phony these people are," I commented.

"It's most disheartening," Timothy answered. "We're being treated disrespectfully just because we declined their offers. I've formed a very negative opinion of Las Vegas over these past few days."

Of the twelve potential customers who missed out on the initial limousine ride, four more reconsidered and were badgered into purchasing a unit after all. That earned them a shared limo ride back to their hotels.

That left eight lonely souls who had successfully resisted all the sales pressure.

An older man approached our table and handed out the meal and show vouchers.

Another half hour passed and finally a small, beat-up van arrived. We were all stuffed inside and driven back to the hotel which had sponsored the tour. It was now four o'clock.

"So much for the promise of a two hour tour," I moaned to Timothy. "It's been almost seven hours since we signed on to take the tour."

"I'm too angry at the moment to contemplate what if anything I learned today," Timothy complained.

"Well, we can get a bit of revenge tonight. Our supper and show are both being paid for by those sleazy Time Share vultures."

As we changed for supper, I arranged a day tour to Laughlin for the following morning using another one of my handy two-for-one coupons.

For our free supper we chose the buffet, which was quite delicious.

The show too was enjoyable, featuring a singer and a comedian whose routine wasn't too vulgar.

After the show Timothy and I took in the eleven o'clock light show and then came right back to our room and hit the sack.

CHAPTER 12 (Cheap Tours and Caveman Keno)

The tour of Laughlin on Wednesday was most
enjoyable.

I had taken it many times in the past but
for Timothy, the experience was awesome.

We drove over the Hoover Dam and later,
while proceeding through the desert, the bus
driver announced that some of the rare Joshua
trees we passed were more than 2,000 years
old.

"My word," Timothy exclaimed, "I'm
stunned. Some of these trees were here at the
time Jesus walked this Earth."

I didn't comment, not wanting my atheistic
or at least agnostic outlook on such matters
to burst his little bubble of happiness.

Bums accosted us in Laughlin.

I refused to put my hand in my wallet but
Timothy gave money to each and every one.

When we got back to our hotel at seven,
despite Timothy's objections, I booked another
tour for the next day to the Grand Canyon.

The priest didn't want me spending so much
money on him, but I had seen how thrilled he
was on today's tour. I assured Timothy that I
hadn't seen the Grand Canyon for at least
thirty years when I was here with Gabriela and
really wanted to go there again. I added that
I had managed to find a last-minute bargain
where I could use another two-for-one voucher.

Although this tour was very long and
tiring, the scenery was breathtaking and well
worth the lengthy bus ride there and back. We
saw the South Rim and had lunch at the lodge
in Grand Canyon Park.

On the bus ride home, Timothy exclaimed
that this had been the most magnificent day of
his life. It pleased me immensely that I had

insisted that we take the tour and that he had loved it so much.

We grabbed a very late supper in the El Cortez coffee shop at ten o'clock shortly after we got back, and then we went to bed exhausted.

It was almost ten o'clock when we finally woke up on Friday morning. Yesterday had been so fatiguing.

We went downstairs and ate a late breakfast.

"This is my last day in Las Vegas," Timothy said. "What shall we do today? I'm still too tired from those tours to do much more walking."

"Exactly how opposed to gambling are you at this moment?" I inquired.

"From what little I've seen, I don't like the way it makes gamblers lie and become aggressive, and I wonder how many of them can really afford to lose as much money as they do. Why do you ask?"

"It would be a travesty to fly all this way to the gambling capital of the world and not lose a single dime. Let's go sit together at a couple of Caveman Keno slot machines here in the El Cortez, and I'll show you how it's possible to gamble without losing your shirt or becoming addicted."

I watched Timothy weigh the pros and cons of my proposal in his mind.

After a moment of contemplation, he acquiesced.

I picked two machines in the quiet rear section of the casino and we sat down side by side.

"You've got to use your own money to gamble," I told Tim. "Put a five dollar bill in this slot."

He did so and his credit meter registered twenty credits.

"Now pick your seven favorite numbers."

The priest thought momentarily before choosing each number.

"Bet one credit, which is twenty-five cents. I'll do the same on my machine."

I explained how the game worked and we began.

On his very first try Timothy hit three of his seven numbers so won his bet back.

"Not bad for your very first foray into the seedy world of gambling," I teased.

After fifteen minutes of betting just one credit at a time, we were still playing on our first five dollars.

"As you can see, my brand of gambling is relatively inexpensive. Drinks are free for gamblers so in the evenings I like to drink beer or Bailey's coffee and slowly get hammered. It's great fun for someone like me who comes to Vegas alone. How do you like it so far?"

"I haven't formed an opinion yet but this form of low-level gambling appears to be both enjoyable and harmless. How do you prevent yourself from getting hooked and upping your bets?"

"That's a very perceptive question. Many people can't do it. I call it the 'EVEN BIGGER JACKPOT THEORY'. People don't get the same thrill the second time they hit the same jackpot, so they keep betting more in the hopes of reliving that initial high. Usually the results are disastrous. I've managed to avoid that pitfall. For one thing, I write down every cent I gamble so I'm able to keep precise track of my losses. Also, being a cheapskate certainly helps me from losing too much. It's the challenge of trying to beat the machines each time I sit down that provides the bulk of my enjoyment. The size of the jackpots is much less of a factor for me."

My credit meter edged its way down to zero, so I put another $5 into the machine and made a notation of same in my little recording notebook.

Timothy was holding his own and still had twenty-two credits. If he quit now he'd be up fifty cents. I was just about to point that out to him when he started chanting "Yes, yes, come on. YES" and then pumped his fist in the air.

His machine rang as his credits got added to the meter.

"Well done," I chuckled. "You hit five out of seven numbers with all three eggs cracked. That's a good jackpot."

"How much did I win?"

"That jackpot earned you thirty bucks. You've now got a total of 122 credits."

"What do you think I should do now?"

"It's up to you. If you continue playing, then you may hit another jackpot, but on the other hand, the machine can take your winnings back mighty quickly."

"That's a typical lawyer's answer which says nothing. You're the gambling expert. Be specific. Shall I stay or shall I go?"

"My sage advice is to play the machine down to 120 credits and then cash in. That means you have two chances to hit a big jackpot. Good luck."

Timothy paused for a moment and then bet one credit. He got nothing so bet the second quarter with the same negative result. He paused for a moment and then hit the "CASH

OUT" button. The machine spit out a ticket for $30.

"Now what do I do?"

"We'll go to the cashier and you can get the cash. Congratulations! You've beaten the casinos on your very first trip to Las Vegas. Not many people can truthfully say that."

We decided to walk slowly around the downtown area just drinking in the atmosphere. At Binion's we got our free picture taken together with a million dollars in cash spread out in front of us. The photos made a nice souvenir.

During our stroll we were accosted by several panhandlers including the fellow we saw the other day who was still wearing an orange shirt, only this time it said "JESUS STILL LOVES YOU". I noticed the subtle change in the message but Tim did not so I didn't mention it to him.

Just like the other day, Timothy and I had gotten separated by ten or fifteen feet when I encountered that particular deadbeat who was sitting on the sidewalk with his back up against a casino wall.

As I got near him, he plaintively asked, "Can you spare a bit of change, sir. I'm flat broke today and I'm very hungry."

"I told you the other day on the Strip to get off your ass and get a job."

"Don't you have even one sympathetic bone in your body for the destitute?" the bum brazenly asked.

"Not for lazy deadbeats like you," I shot back as I continued on past him.

When I glanced around looking for Timothy, the priest was again opening his wallet and handing money over to the Jesus freak while chatting with him.

When Timothy caught up to me, I chastised him.

"That was the same bum we saw the other day near the Fashion Show Mall. I told you these people make a career out of scamming the tourists. Even worse, surely you realize that the young woman with the red bandana around her head earlier was a drug addict. That five bucks you handed her is going to get shot right into her arm. Throwing money at these deadbeats makes you nothing but an enabler. They'll never get off the streets so long as suckers like you with good intentions keep funding their laziness."

"It's better to err on the side of mercy, Boyd. Each of the individuals who approached me needs the money far more than I do. My religion stresses sharing."

"One of us isn't seeing the bigger picture. If you tried handing a sandwich to these losers instead of cash, I think you'd be shocked at their response."

"I'm sorry Boyd, but I can't in good conscience refuse them. Speaking of which, would you mind staying up in our hotel room this evening after supper? I'd like to hash over certain issues with you without the distraction of the casino noise during our final night together."

"Sure, that'll be fine so long as we can drink beer while we're talking."

We ate in the El Cortez coffee shop using one of my two-for-one coupons while our beer was chilling on ice in our wastebasket upstairs.

When we got up to our room after the meal, the first thing I did was order a shuttle bus pickup for nine o'clock the next morning as

well as a wake-up call for seven. Timothy's
flight departed the next day at noon.

CHAPTER 13 (Lawyer Versus Priest)

Timothy sat on the sofa and I pulled the soft armchair over on the other side of the coffee table so that we were facing each other.

We cracked open our first beer.

Timothy took a long swig from his can and said, "You're something of an enigma to me. Your generosity in allowing me, a total stranger, to share your hotel room, and your insistence on paying for virtually all my expenses other than my gifts to panhandlers, is remarkable. I realize that you're extremely wealthy but you don't act like it. In fact your frugality is quite amusing and you don't put on airs. On the other hand, you appear unreasonably hard-hearted in your response to the plight of the less fortunate, and you hinted the other day that you're some sort of predatory con-man, attending various church services for the sole purpose of finding trusting widows to fleece. Are you in fact a dishonest attorney?"

I pondered the question for a moment while I collected my thoughts. The priest was treating this conversation most seriously. This was not the time for flippancy.

"No one considers himself to be a crook, Timothy. We all find ways to justify whatever we do. I don't blatantly steal from my clients or misappropriate money from my trust accounts. Instead I charge my clients, virtually all of whom are rich, top dollar to handle their legal affairs, which I might add, I complete with absolute accuracy and with as much speed as our legal system allows."

"Are you saying that you overcharge them?"

"Indirectly perhaps, but I'm very upfront about my legal fees. Sure, the little old ladies could easily find another lawyer who would act as their Estate Trustee for a fraction of what I charge, but I don't really deceive my clients. I've simply got the gift of gab coupled with the look of a kindly old lawyer. That combination is tough for the old dears to resist."

"What exactly does an Estate Trustee have to do?" the priest asked.

"I'm not sure what you call it in America. The former term we used in Canada was 'Executor', and it entails preparing an inventory of the estate, selling everything that hasn't been specifically given to a beneficiary, and then dividing up the cash among the various beneficiaries. Being the Estate Trustee is entirely separate from doing the legal work on an estate, which is performed by an attorney and involves preparing the various legal forms required before the Estate Trustee can distribute the assets to the heirs."

"Does that mean that you're double dipping with your fees?" Timothy inquired.

"You're very perceptive, Timothy. That's exactly what I do. Doing the legal work is moderately lucrative but being the Estate Trustee is a bonanza of easy money."

"Do you disclose that your services could be secured elsewhere at a substantially reduced cost?"

"Of course not! Does Wal-Mart tell its customers that an item is much cheaper over at Target? It's up to the clients to shop around before purchasing something. Besides, in my experience, most lawyers who undercharge for their time don't provide high quality results."

"Then explain to me why you consider yourself to be a predator who cheats his clients?"

I paused for a moment while I decided how to respond.

"Think back to those Time Share people from the other day. They omitted mentioning the rather onerous yearly costs of maintaining a unit and were most evasive when the subject was raised. In some ways I'm probably similar to them although I don't think I like the comparison one bit."

"I'm not quite following you," Timothy interjected.

"Just like those salesmen, I've got a series of tried and tested lines that I use to hook the clients. I mention how their deaths often bring out complete and destructive dissension in their families as the various beneficiaries begin fighting about everything. I stress that all that trouble can be eliminated by having a trusted third party, such as me, act as the Estate Trustee. I go on to compare the standard 5 percent trustee fee to the commission a real estate agent earns to sell their home, but emphasize that estates are excruciatingly complicated these days what with tax issues and all. I also highlight the fact that I've been specializing in estate work for most of my long legal career and that my reputation is impeccable."

"That doesn't sound at all underhanded," the priest responded. "In fact it seems like wise advice."

"Well, it's mostly a load of crap. In reality the main beneficiaries, or at least a couple of them, should be the Estate Trustees.

90

For one thing, that keeps the huge trustee fee in the pockets of the main heirs where it belongs. Besides, the lawyer doing the estate legal work can always step up to settle any arguments. The bottom line is that I don't put my clients' interests as my primary goal. Instead I look after myself first and foremost. That's a bit embarrassing to admit but I know that it's true and it's made me rich."

"You threw out the figure of $600,000 as your annual income derived from a scant twenty hour work week. To someone like me, that sounds obscene. Have you considered reducing your estate fees in order to benefit your clients?"

"No; my reasoning has been that my clients are wealthy and don't need special bargains. Look Timothy, as I've gotten to know you over the past week, I've concluded that you're close to saintly. Giving your life savings to some deadbeat family so they didn't get evicted immediately was far beyond mere generosity. I've developed the highest admiration for you personally and have come to believe that you're a genuinely altruistic individual. But with all due respect, since you're a Catholic priest, you're the last person who should be criticizing me for my tactics."

"I don't understand. What does my church have to do with this discussion?"

"Face the truth, Timothy, your church and I are both in the lucrative business of milking widows in order to maximize our profits."

Timothy leapt up, his face red with anger, as he shouted, "You're so incredibly wrong! Your nonsense is blasphemous! My church does nothing but good works. How dare you malign it!"

"Look, Timothy, if this subject is too sensitive for you, we don't have to pursue it. It's unlikely we're going to find any common ground anyway."

The priest sat back down.

"I'm sorry for raising my voice, Boyd. Let me rephrase what I said. I strongly disagree with your point of view, but I'm willing to sit here calmly while you explain why you said it. Please proceed."

"Fair enough, but I think we need another beer."

I went over to the wastebasket and extracted another cold can of beer for each of us while I pondered whether I should disclose my opinion about his church or drop the subject.

Comparing myself to the Time Share thieves had already upset me. Verbalizing the vague guilt that I had successfully kept buried about how I ran my law practice was already beginning to make me ashamed of myself.

I decided not to upset Timothy by criticizing his Catholic Church. He seemed completely happy and content with his chosen career and it wasn't the place of a slick lawyer to raise any doubts in the mind of such a dedicated priest.

"I've changed my mind, Tim. My warped views are probably pure garbage anyway. Let's talk about something else."

"You're not getting away that easily, Boyd. You insulted my church and I'm entitled to a full explanation. It's rare for a priest to find anyone who is willing to speak his mind, and I need to know exactly why you believe the Catholic Church takes advantage of its elderly parishioners."

"Very well, Timothy, if you insist. I've done hundreds of estates over the course of my career and drafted thousands of Wills. You may not realize it, but all the churches including yours put great pressure on my little old lady clients to be generous to the church when drafting their Wills. Don't try to tell me that when you visit the elderly in their homes or in the hospital, you don't encourage them to bequeath money freely to your Catholic Church."

"I hear what you're saying, Boyd, but when I do suggest a donation or bequest, it's the good works which would arise out of the gift that motivates me."

"Answer me truthfully, Tim. Does your church train you how to increase the weekly offerings from the faithful as well as how to persuade them to remember the church I their Wills?"

The priest blushed and then smiled.

"You may have a bit of a valid point. I have attended seminars designed to teach us how to promote generous giving to the church both before and after death."

"With over two thousand years of practice under its belt, I'm certain that the Catholic Church has developed lines that beat my own legal baloney by a country mile. Your church has become astoundingly rich in the process. In fact I've even heard some of your church's clever entreaties directly from my clients when we were discussing their Wills."

"I disagree with your allegations, Boyd. I've never related those seminars directly with church profits, and I've certainly never had any monetary motivations in my dealings with parishioners. Since you run your own business, then perhaps I can understand how you might equate donations with profits. I certainly can confirm that it's quite costly to run a parish and carry out God's work."

"It's not nearly as costly as it should be," I retorted.

"What do you mean?"

"I can understand a devout person like you working ungodly hours for peanuts and living in poverty. You do it for the good of humanity. But I can't forgive your employer for treating you like a slave."

That statement angered the priest.

"I'm no slave," he bellowed. "I'm a priest who has happily and willingly dedicated his life to God. I live like I do so that I can serve others, improve this world for the downtrodden, and please God."

"I believe you, Timothy. You're not the problem. It's the Catholic Church that's grossly in the wrong here. They're treating you terribly. Your education is at least as extensive as mine and all professionals should be fairly paid. Most other churches pay their clergy well. Your church works you to the bone for a tiny fraction of your true monetary worth. Caring people denounce multinational corporations for paying starvation wages to offshore workers in order to increase profits. Your church does precisely the same thing to its priests and nuns. It's criminal."

The priest was silent for several seconds.

"I'm glad we had this conversation, Boyd. Even if I disagree entirely with your analysis, it's a point of view I've never considered before. Travel obviously does broaden the mind, and you've given me ample food for thought on my journey home tomorrow."

We changed the topic and reminisced about the past week in Las Vegas. Then we talked about our lives growing up and many other less weighty issues while we sipped more beer.

Just before Timothy retired to his little bedroom, I opined, "Wouldn't it be interesting if both of us were partly right?"

"It would," Timothy answered. "I also wonder if God caused our paths to cross, not to save me from a week of homelessness, but to allow us to share such diverse perspectives."

CHAPTER 14 (Another Rescue)

Timothy and I had an early breakfast downstairs and then I waited with him at the El Cortez main entrance until his airport shuttle arrived.

It was damn chilly outside. A massive cold front had moved in to Las Vegas overnight and, combined with a bitter wind, had turned the summer weather into winter.

Timothy refused my offer of money and insisted that he had sufficient funds to get himself safely home.

We promised to stay in touch and he thanked me again for looking after him so well.

We shook hands just before he stepped onto the bus. Real men don't hug.

I went back to my room to get a jacket and then I walked over to the Plaza and confirmed my reservation for six nights beginning tomorrow.

For the rest of the day I flitted from casino to casino using my player's cards in each establishment. That strategy tended to keep the free offers and special promotions coming in the mail or on-line.

I had never gambled so little on a vacation here. I was only down $40 as of this morning even though I hadn't experienced a single winning session. Spending so much time showing the priest around had certainly saved me more money than I had spent feeding and entertaining him.

Not only that, but I realized that having company had greatly enhanced my vacation. The companionship and discussions had been most enjoyable and thought-provoking.

While I distractedly played Caveman Keno at the various casinos, I began pondering what type of lawyer and person I had become since Gabriela had passed away.

Although I didn't reach any definite conclusions, the disquieting notion formed that Father Timothy and Jim Corbett were much better human beings than I was.

It appeared that ever since Gabriela's death so many years ago, I had transformed myself into a cold money-making automaton, selfish, opinionated and miserly.

I couldn't fathom why I had shunned all romantic relationships since my wife had died. I hadn't been out on a single date and I was close to no one except Corbett. I formed the nagging suspicion that I had lived alone solely to keep my wealth safe from possible marital confiscation. That harsh pre-judgment of the true motives of women had resulted in a quarter-century of loneliness.

It was a very sobering self-assessment.

My luck on the slots was moderately dismal and by six o'clock I had lost $60. As I walked from the Las Vegas Club toward the Fremont, I spotted a shivering bum huddled against the wall and about to hit me up for a handout.

The wide pedestrian walkway was virtually empty as this sudden cold weather had driven most people indoors.

As I steeled myself to ignore the pest, he began his worn-out spiel.

"Excuse me, sir. I'm so hungry and cold right now. Could you please spare a bit of change so I can get something to eat?"

There was something in his voice which resonated with me.

Instead of barging past him with or without a rude comment, I found myself stopping and reaching into my pocket for some coins.

Even though the man's breath had the unmistakable odor of booze, I asked "Where are you from?"

"Copper Hill, Tennessee. I've lived in Las Vegas for the past few months but haven't been able to find work. I'm flat broke now and completely desperate."

I put the loose change from my pocket into his shivering hands.

"Why are you wearing a short-sleeved shirt? Haven't you noticed that it's freezing out here?"

"The whole world's been against me lately. I got evicted from my rooming house a few days ago and someone stole my clothes last night while I was sleeping behind a boarded-up house. Now all I've got is what's on my back."

"That's an effective line, buddy. On the off-chance that it's true, this is your lucky day because I'm in an unusually generous mood. How much will it take to get you a roof over your head for a few nights and some cheap clothes?"

The chap, who was likely in his early thirties, peered into my eyes, probably wondering what the catch was.

"I know a spot where I can get a room for a whole week for $99 plus tax," he replied.

"Fair enough chum," I said as I counted out some cash. "Here's $210. Go get yourself something to eat, buy some warmer clothes and put that roof over your head for the next week. Good luck to you. I hope your string of bad luck is officially over now."

His eyes widened in amazement as he snatched the money of my hand.

"I can't thank you enough, sir. You have no idea how much this means to me."

He scurried away and I continued into the Fremont where I cashed a traveler's check to replenish my lost cash.

I smiled to myself when I realized that Father Timothy had just cost me over two hundred bucks. It must have been his influence that made me open my wallet. Oddly, I felt a distinct twinge of pride in what I had just done.

Within an hour I had lost another $15 on the slots. My daily gambling limit of $75 had now been used up so I braved the cold again as I walked back to the El Cortez to have supper.

By now it was dark outside and had gotten even more blustery.

I was wearing a short-sleeved shirt, a long-sleeved sweatshirt over it plus a thin windbreaker I had won with a jackpot several years earlier, but despite the multiple layers of clothing, I wished that I had brought a hat and gloves on this trip. I hadn't expected to encounter such cold weather here in April so had packed light clothing only.

I picked up my pace because of the wind and cold, not wishing to spend any more time than necessary outside.

Instead of walking down Fremont Street all the way to the El Cortez, I decided to take a short cut through a little parkette which ran from Las Vegas Boulevard to the main east entrance of my hotel.

This small park was quite new and had been constructed with top quality decorative paving stones. There were several palm trees interspersed with two or three small benches which were just big enough for two people to

sit on but designed in such a way that the
bums couldn't sleep on them.

The park was fairly well lit and I wasn't
concerned about getting mugged.

The place was virtually empty when I
entered, with just one person sitting on a
bench at the far end.

As I got nearer I noticed that it was an
elderly woman on the bench and that she had
one of those small airline bags with wheels
and an extendable handle.

Knowing that Vegas was full of crazies who
just wanted to be left alone, I walked by
silently, determined to mind my own business.

Out of the corner of my eye I noticed that
the old woman was shivering. She definitely
wasn't dressed warmly enough to keep out this
bitter cold.

I left the park and crossed the street.
Just as I was about to enter the El Cortez, a
twinge of guilt tweaked my conscience and I
stopped dead in my tracks pondering what
Timothy would do in this situation.

One part of my mind urged me to get my ass
out of the cold but another small voice buried
deep in the recesses of my brain whispered
that I should help the woman or at least
determine if she needed assistance.

A bit peeved with myself for even
bothering, I turned around and crossed the
street back to the park where I walked toward
the lady.

This was an old woman, at least eighty,
and something definitely didn't add up.

"Good evening, ma'am. Excuse my intrusion,
but it seems far too cold to be sitting
outside."

"I guess I hadn't noticed," she replied
softly.

"I can't help but see that you have an airline bag with you. Are you waiting for your room to be ready at the El Cortez?"

She shook her head.

"Please don't think that I'm being nosy, but do you mind telling me why you're sitting here alone in the cold after dark?"

"I guess not. I'm in a pickle and don't really know what to do about it."

"Look, I'm a lawyer from Canada and I'm perfectly harmless. Why don't we go into the hotel where it's warm? I haven't had my supper yet so I'll treat you to a bite to eat and you can tell me all about your problem. I'm pretty good at listening."

"It's not your problem, it's mine."

"Fine, you old bat," I muttered silently to myself. "You can sit out here all night and catch pneumonia or get mugged if that's what you want. Why did I even bother to waste my time? It's that damn Timothy's fault. Don't tell me I'm growing a conscience."

That other little voice again overrode my cynical side and chastised me by saying, "If you can get some widow to trust you with her entire fortune, surely you can persuade this pathetic old woman to come in out of the cold."

I decided to turn on the charm.

"My name's Boyd Billingsworth and I'm here in Las Vegas on vacation staying at the El Cortez. What's your name?"

She told me that her name was Beatrice Laundry but she liked to be called Bea.

"Where are you from, Bea?"

"A little place called Ozona, Texas."

"Really! Believe it or not, I've actually been there. Years ago on a driving trip I spent a night at a motel in Ozona. The reason

I still remember is because the owner's cat took a liking to me for some reason. It snuck into my room and wouldn't leave. Despite my normal dislike of cats, I let it sit on my lap while I drank beer, and later I let it sleep on the bed with me. Since I was alone on that trip, I actually enjoyed the companionship."

That tidbit of trivia got the old girl's attention.

"Do you remember which motel you stayed at?"

"I think the name was the Hillcrest Motel or something like that. There was a restaurant right across the road and I ate supper there and also breakfast the next morning."

"What a small world!" Bea exclaimed. "I used to be a maid in that motel and I also worked part-time as a waitress in the diner. Do you recall what year you were there?"

"Let me think. I guess it must have been in early February of 1993."

"That's amazing. I worked in the motel back then and I even remember that cat. Its name was Little Grey and I had a devil of a time keeping it out of the rooms when I was making them up. It kept sneaking in and gave me fits trying to shoo it back outside."

"That is a fascinating coincidence, Bea. Look, I'd love to hear more about Ozona and that motel. Let's go into the El Cortez, warm up and I'll treat us to supper. I'm starved."

That personal connection with the cat melted the old girl's resistance and she consented to dine with me.

I offered to carry her little bag but Bea insisted on pulling it herself.

We walked across the street and into the hotel. I could tell that she was glad to get in out of the cold.

Bea said that she needed to go to the bathroom but wouldn't leave her bag with me. She lugged it in behind her.

I had no idea what her problem might be and I was amazed that I had bothered to go back and chat with her. It was so out of character.

When Bea emerged I suggested that we eat in the coffee shop at the rear of the casino. The hostess seated us at a table near the back and we ordered coffee right away.

"I won't let you spend your hard-earned money on an old woman like me," Bea said stubbornly. "All I want is the coffee."

Somehow I suspected that she wasn't being truthful so I resorted to one of my cunning legal ploys.

"What a shame, Bea! I've got this fantastic two-for-one coupon which I've got to use up before it expires. Normally I eat alone. This was going to be my one chance to finally get the casino to repay me a pittance for all the money I've lost here. Will you please reconsider? Your supper won't cost me a cent."

Who could resist such a line?

"In that case I'd love to get some food," Bea admitted. "I actually haven't eaten anything since a bit of breakfast early this morning."

We each ordered the hot beef sandwich with gravy and fries.

When the waitress brought our coffee and left with our food order, I said, "Okay, Bea, tell me all about this pickle you find yourself in."

"I guess I'm just a silly old fool," she began. "I'm eighty-six years young and until today I'd never been out of west Texas. I've been widowed since 1984 and money has always been hard to come by in my little home town. Three weeks ago I was watching a TV show about Las Vegas and it seemed so magnificent that I decided I wanted to visit here before I die."

Just then the waitress returned with our soup which was included with our dinners. Bea paused so that we could eat the soup while it was still hot.

"Please continue your story," I said once she had finished her soup.

"I bought a plane ticket from Dallas to Las Vegas from the local travel agent, arriving today and returning on Tuesday. I also purchased a return bus ticket from Ozona to Dallas at the variety store which serves as our bus station. Unfortunately I wasn't able to arrange a hotel through the agency because the prices were all too high. I decided that I'd have no trouble finding a cheap motel once I got here."

I smiled to myself, realizing that Bea had put herself in the same tight corner as Timothy by hitting Vegas on one of its busiest weeks.

She carried on explaining what had occurred.

"Really early this morning I caught the bus from Ozona to Dallas and had plenty of time to catch my flight. I had never been on an airplane and found the whole experience tremendously exciting. I got to talking to a man sitting beside me on the plane, and he said I'd never be able to find a room on the Strip that I could afford."

"How much were you hoping to pay for a room?" I queried.

"No more than $50 per night. When I told the man that, he suggested that I try the downtown area and he told me about the cheap shuttle buses. When I got off the plane I caught a bus downtown."

The waitress arrived with our entrees, so we paused in order to eat our suppers. Bea tackled her meal like a duck going after a June bug. She had definitely been very hungry.

Finally Bea came up for air and continued with her story.

"Another couple got off at a hotel called the Plaza a few blocks from here, so I followed them into the hotel and waited in line at the registration desk. It was about three o'clock by then. When it was my turn to be served, the lady told me that they were booked solid tonight and so was their sister hotel across the street. I was starting to get worried. I had no idea it would be so tough to find a room in such a huge city."

Bea let out a big sigh.

"That's when things turned from bad to worse. I went back outside and started walking toward another hotel I saw just up the road. I got about halfway there when I realized that I was exhausted and needed to rest. I hadn't walked so far in years and I was pulling my little suitcase along behind me all the while. Do you really want to hear any more?"

"I do, Bea. Please go on."

"I sat down on a bench to rest my feet and I put my purse down beside me while I took off my shoes. My feet were killing me and I just needed to sit for a bit. I didn't notice anyone walking by me, but I may have dozed off for a moment. When I went to put my shoes back on and reached for my purse, it was gone."

Up to that point I had been listening intently and believed every word.

However, as soon as Bea mentioned the lost purse, I immediately became suspicious. My natural lawyer's distrust of humanity kicked in and I scolded myself for butting into this old woman's affairs.

"Serves you right," the lawyer's side of my brain taunted. "Now this old con artist is going to hit you up for some money. What a sucker you are!"

My mind drifted back to the mid 1980's when Gabriela and I were staying at Bally's on the Strip. I was out walking alone and waiting for a light to change. This was long before the city constructed the overhead pedestrian walkways at the main intersections.

An older lady in a wheelchair asked if I would help her get across the busy road. When the light changed and I began pushing her, she related a tale of woe about losing her purse and finding herself broke and stranded, waiting for her daughter to arrive in a couple of days to rescue her.

Although I was quite cynical even back then, I did feel sympathy for this poor woman and had almost convinced myself to give her ample money to get a hotel room and some meals. Suddenly my memory dredged up a tidbit from the day before.

I recalled walking behind a young couple pushing a lady in a wheelchair, and I overheard her give them an eerily similar sob story. In a flash I realized that the woman was a huckster, preying on the goodwill of tourists to make some easy money.

When we reached the other side of the street, I wished the lady good luck but gave her nothing.

Back then I attended church regularly with Gabriela for all the right reasons, not to

pick up rich clients. I remembered thinking
that if it turned out that I was wrong about
the woman, then I'd likely rot in Hell for my
coldness. The next day, however, I saw the
same lady lurking on the same intersection
plying her con game.

Bea's story was remarkably similar to that
of the lady in the wheelchair. Could it be
that Bea had been sitting in the little park
like a spider waiting for a gullible fly to
wander by?

Bea was continuing with her story.

"I walked back to the Plaza and they
called the police for me. The young officer
was very polite and took down my name and
address but told me it was very unlikely that
my purse would ever be found. He did take me
back to the bench and then he looked around
that area just in case the thief had taken out
my money and dumped the purse, but the
policeman found nothing. Suddenly he received
an emergency call and had to rush off. He gave
me his precinct business card so I could check
in later in case my purse gets turned in."

"After the officer left, I felt just awful
and foolish and old. I wandered around
downtown and eventually spotted that little
park you found me in."

"My plane and bus tickets are in my little
suitcase as well as my passport, but my
driver's license and all my money were in the
purse. I've never owned a credit card. I've
only got about $30 left in my bank account
back home until my social security gets
deposited at the end of the month."

"And that's the pickle I now find myself
in. Have you ever heard of anything so
stupid?"

My mind was racing, arguing back and forth with itself.

The lawyer in me was screaming, "Run, run. Pay for the old huckster's supper and give her twenty bucks. Scam alert! Scam alert!"

My human side was much kinder. "Just a minute; you approached this poor woman, not the other way around. She couldn't have been sitting in that park looking for a sucker. It hardly gets used after dark. The only thing she would have found there was trouble. You told her you'd listen. Now help her out. Don't abandon her."

I looked at Beatrice for a moment trying to decide what to do. Finally I decided to give her the benefit of the doubt.

"What a terrible way to start your holiday, Bea! Were you planning on sitting in the cold on that park bench until next Tuesday?"

"I wasn't really thinking at all. I was just in a daze. The whole day has been so strange. Some problems are just too big to deal with, and I'm so beat right now, I don't know whether I'm coming or going."

"I know that the El Cortez is booked solid tonight," I said. "The slot tournaments have drawn record numbers to Las Vegas for the past two weekends. I expect that a lot of rooms will be available tomorrow night because the tournaments will end this evening."

I paused again to further collect my thoughts.

"Strangely enough, Bea, you're not the only tourist who got surprised by the fully occupied hotels. Last Sunday I encountered a Catholic priest from southeast Texas who was in almost the same boat as you are now. He couldn't find a room and hadn't brought nearly enough money with him. This hotel put a portable cot in my room and the priest stayed with me all week until he flew home this morning. For tonight, you're perfectly welcome to use that cot."

"Oh, thank you, but I couldn't possibly stay in a hotel room with a strange man," Bea replied in horror.

"It's not as disreputable as it sounds, Bea. My room is actually a suite and the cot is in its own little room with a secure door to close. It's the perfect solution for your problem tonight. Tomorrow I'm sure I can find you your own room."

Bea didn't respond and I suddenly realized how drained she looked.

"Tell you what, Bea. Come upstairs and I'll show you the layout. If it seems proper, then you can go right to bed and get some sleep. You look like you're about ready to drop."

After a moment of reflection, Beatrice relented and we made our way up to the room. She inspected the cot and the door to the tiny room and decided that the layout was acceptable.

"Is it okay with you if I go to bed right now?" she asked plaintively.

"Of course, Bea; have a great sleep and I'm sure everything will seem much more manageable in the morning."

She thanked me for being so kind and generous, and we said goodnight.

...

The second week of my vacation was remarkably similar to the first week.

The following day, being Sunday, I got
Beatrice her own room in the Plaza on the same
floor as mine. I was even able to use some of
my player's points to get a great rate on her
room.

I rented a car and drove Bea to Red Rock
Canyon as well as up and down the Strip. I
also made her purchase a new purse and a few
other needed items that had been stolen.

On Monday I treated her to a bus trip to
Laughlin, which she absolutely adored.

On Tuesday I rode the shuttle bus with her
to the airport and ensured that she got her
boarding pass. Despite Bea's objections, I
made her take $200 in cash to tide her over
until her social security came in.

She hugged me just before she went through
security and expressed her eternal gratitude.

I had successfully carried out another
rescue.

The rest of the week was quiet. I actually
hit a couple of half-decent slot jackpots and
wound up with a trip gambling profit of $80.

When I reached the Syracuse airport late
on Saturday night, I was too tired to begin
the three hour drive back to Belleville, so I
stayed at the same hotel where Little Chevy
had been parked.

On Sunday morning, which was Easter, I
drove home, highly satisfied with my entire
holiday and proud that I hadn't been rude to a
single normal person since first meeting
Father Timothy in the Houston airport. The
only creatures who had been made to endure my
acerbic comments since then were some of the
aggressive panhandlers.

The priest had certainly been a maturing
influence on me.

## CHAPTER 15 (Questioning Authority)

Father Timothy looked out the window of the airplane and thanked God for looking after him so well in Las Vegas. Everything had worked out marvelously and Timothy had even met a new friend.

His conversations with the lawyer were nagging at Timothy so deeply that he couldn't even concentrate on the scenery far below.

Boyd had called Timothy a slave to a predatory, greedy and abusive employer.

Had Timothy really aided and abetted in the fleecing of lonely devout parishioners?

He had certainly never perceived it in that light, always believing that his bedside requests for generosity to the Catholic Church were made simply to further the works of God.

It was somewhat shocking to realize that a self-described avaricious and cunning attorney viewed churches as having similar scurrilous motives to his own.

Boyd's admission that he stalked elderly women at church services for the sole purpose of getting his hands on their wealth bordered on pure evil.

Surely Timothy hadn't been unwittingly doing the same thing on his rounds to the shut-ins and to those in hospital.

What a dreadful thought!

Once the plane landed in Houston, Timothy made his way to the main bus depot for the final leg of his homeward journey. His own financial circumstances suddenly troubled him greatly. His bank account was effectively empty until his next payday at the end of the month.

At least there was ample food in his pantry and refrigerator to carry him through, but he'd have to go easy on the beer and wine.

Perhaps giving so much money to save Maria's family from eviction hadn't been wise after all. Timothy suspected that his new-found lawyer friend was probably correct. Maria would likely be facing the same dire situation in a few months, possibly even earlier.

Surely the diocese would reimburse Timothy for the money he had spent to rescue his desperate parishioners.

He certainly didn't want to turn into a distrusting cynic like the lawyer, blaming the poor for their own plight.

Tomorrow would be busy with the Sunday masses and the backlog of visits and assorted parish problems which would inevitably have arisen during Timothy's absence.

The archbishop's office had been irritated with Timothy for taking this vacation so close to the upcoming Holy Week. He had hoped to be spared the task of the Sunday masses this weekend, but his superiors would have none of that. Tonight's five o'clock mass had been cancelled because of Timothy's holiday since no other priest in the area could be coerced into performing the service and there was no way Timothy could ensure that he was back in Bleakwood in time for the mass.

Monday would also be an ordeal coping with the annual visit of the Archbishop and his demanding assistant. They were eternally trying to cut costs and this time here was Timothy seeking reimbursement for his major expenditure on Maria's family.

Timothy's performance review was also to be carried out at the same time in private with the Archbishop. Those meetings were always stressful and usually belittling as Timothy was perennially being chastised for falling short with his weekly offering targets. It wasn't Timothy's fault that his parishioners were generally poor and unable to donate generously to their church.

Eventually the bus dropped the priest off in Kirbyville where he had left the church's old vehicle the week before.

The old clunker wouldn't start at first and Timothy was worried that he might have to walk the five miles to Bleakwood, but finally he managed to get it started and nursed it home.

It was after ten o'clock and pitch black outside by the time Timothy entered his housing quarters adjacent to the church.

Sunday was a nightmare. The volunteer church treasurer spent three tedious hours with Timothy after the final mass explaining the financial statements for the latest fiscal period.

That evening was taken up with three visits to sick parishioners.

Timothy only had time for a couple of beer before he collapsed from exhaustion onto his bed.

Archbishop Murphy and his assistant arrived promptly at ten on Monday morning as scheduled.

"Offerings are down 5 percent," were the first words uttered by Father Bruce, the Archbishop's executive assistant. "That means costs will have to be trimmed by roughly $5,000 to make up the shortfall."

The tone of voice accompanying that terse pronouncement immediately got Timothy's dander up and stirred a rebellion inside of him which must have been dormant but festering in his subconscious.

Timothy had always been meek and mild, forever accommodating and acquiescent to any and all requests or demands.

This time the words of Boyd Billingsworth tauntingly calling Timothy a pathetic slave suddenly made the priest fed up with the way he was being treated.

"There's no room to cut," he barked back, "unless you want me to start baking the communion wafers to save a few pennies. Perhaps you've invented a way to stretch the day into thirty hours. I'm already overworked and sick of being coerced into taking on duties which should be handled by others."

The Archbishop, who had been preoccupied reading the financial statements, glanced up when he detected anger and sarcasm emanating from the mouth of this normally docile priest.

Father Bruce was also suddenly on guard. He hadn't expected any resistance from this perpetually servile veteran cleric.

"The money has to come from somewhere, Father Timothy. We can't run a deficit. I've come up with a few proposals to bring your books back into balance for the current fiscal year."

Timothy sat in silence so Father Bruce continued.

"The diocese has done a cost study of the bus passes we've been providing and this parish doesn't justify that expense. Your own pass will therefore expire at the end of this month. Do you have any comments or concerns regarding that?"

"No, Father Bruce, I agree with your analysis. I only use the pass three or four times a year."

"It's costing over $2,000 annually to cut the lawn and perform the other required yard work," Father Bruce continued. "We propose that you handle that responsibility yourself for the remainder of this fiscal year or find a parishioner willing to do the work for free. Notice of termination has already been delivered to the local contractor."

"Preposterous!" Timothy bellowed. "Five years ago you took away my part-time secretary, which foisted all the correspondence duties onto my shoulders. You assured me it was temporary but I'm still handling all those tasks. Two years ago you postponed hiring a new church custodian after old Harry retired, promising again that it would only be for one year. I have to spend my own time cleaning the pews after each mass and keeping the rectory office clean. I've had to learn how to be a general handyman in order to make ongoing repairs or obtain your reluctant approval to call in a qualified serviceman. These are old buildings. They need proper ongoing maintenance that I'm not capable of handling. How much longer do you intend to postpone replacing Harry? Now you want me to cut the lawn and pull the weeds. There just isn't enough time in my already overstuffed days."

"I'm sure many of your flock would be willing to help out their church for free," the Archbishop interjected.

Timothy didn't have the nerve to contradict Archbishop Murphy even though parishioners willing to perform such tasks were frustratingly rare.

Father Bruce continued.

"We're afraid that you'll have to make do with your current automobile for another year.

115

The diocese can't justify replacing the vehicle at this time."

Timothy was seething inside.

With a steely tone, he explained, "The car you provide for me was already five years old when you assigned it to this parish, and now I've been using it for seven full years. It's got over 200,000 miles on it and is regularly threatening to quit. Twice in the past few months it conked out at night while I was on visitation and it had to be towed. I've been walking as much as possible in an effort to help the old car last. For the past two years you've sat in this very office and assured me that I'd be assigned a newer vehicle the following year. I was really looking forward to getting a set of reliable wheels like you promised."

Timothy always had an atrocious sense of timing when raising monetary issues.

He used the momentary silence of Father Bruce to raise the matter of reimbursement for the money Timothy had spent rescuing Maria's family from eviction.

Timothy handed over the receipt from the landlord and launched into his plea.

"I left three urgent messages with your office on the Friday just before I left on vacation, but you never responded. As I explained in those messages, I was faced with an emergency decision to save one of our church families from immediate eviction. Since I didn't hear from you and time was of the essence, I paid that money out of my own savings. I'm now flat broke and respectfully request reimbursement for the $1,200 I was forced to expend."

Timothy noticed Father Bruce glance over at the Archbishop and raise his eyebrows, which suggested that the two men had already made their decision before they even arrived in Bleakwood.

Father Bruce confirmed the official bad news.

"We're sorry, Father Timothy, but you've been warned in the past about incurring unauthorized expenses. You should have left the matter to the appropriate government agencies. The church won't reimburse you. Hopefully the parishioners will pay you back in due course."

Before Timothy had a chance to respond, Archbishop Murphy stood up and announced that the financial portion of the meeting had to end because of time restraints.

"Father Bruce, kindly go wait in the car while I complete Father Timothy's annual performance review. I'll be out in a few minutes so that we still have time to get to our next appointment on schedule."

The Archbishop began by apologizing for the fiscal restraint that Timothy's parish was forced to endure.

"The church understands how large a burden is being placed on its priests and sisters, Father Timothy, but attendance and offerings are slowly eroding as an aging church-going populace dies off. Your continuing sacrifices are greatly appreciated, and both the church and I are fully satisfied with the quality of your work."

As the Archbishop stood up to leave, Timothy realized that the church was ignoring all of his objections to the cost cutting. It was worse than offensive. Every decision had already been made without first hearing any input from Timothy even though he was the person most affected by the changes.

"Your Holiness, I appeal to you. There's no way I can run this entire church by myself. I'm perpetually exhausted as it is. Postponing a more reliable car for another year I guess I can live with, but doing the yard work is going too far. I'm not a slave and I refuse to be treated like one."

The Archbishop's face darkened with anger.

"That's no attitude to flaunt, Father Camacho, and I'm shocked to hear you complain like this. If you had managed to increase your collections, we'd be rewarding you now, but you failed. Those lost funds have to be made up somewhere."

The Archbishop abruptly stood up and began to leave the room. That just made Timothy more frustrated.

"How can you possibly call this a proper performance review?" Timothy asked sarcastically. "I've got real concerns I need to discuss with you."

"I don't have the time today, Father Camacho," the Archbishop replied icily. "I can't be late for my next meeting."

"But Archbishop, I find that I'm burned out, perpetually lonely and I'm drinking far too much. Last week I spent my vacation in Las Vegas where I met a wealthy Canadian lawyer. We had disturbing conversations about the priesthood and the Catholic Church, and I came away believing that he had made some valid criticisms about the way priests are treated. I need to address those issues."

"The personal demons you mention are serious and need to be addressed. Call my office tomorrow morning and set up an appointment with either me or the diocesan counselor. It's best to nip these negative feelings in the bud. As concerns this attorney from Canada, never believe a word that slithers out of the mouth of a lawyer. They are the scourge of this planet and have caused our church untold misery these past few decades. Good day, Father Camacho."

On Tuesday morning Timothy called the Archbishop's office in Lufkin. Father Bruce took the call and advised that the Archbishop was unavailable. Timothy stressed that he needed to talk about his depression and doubts with the Archbishop as soon as possible.

Father Bruce promised that he would give the message to Archbishop Murphy and then transferred the call to the diocesan counselor's office.

The next available appointment was not until early September.

Timothy booked it anyway but felt abandoned, alone and confused.

CHAPTER 16 (A Complete Change of Heart)

I arrived home at one o'clock on Easter Sunday afternoon, April 20th, after stopping at the post office to pick up my personal mail which I only received at my private post office box.

There was a constant danger in permitting staff to glimpse into one's personal life, so I kept such matters out of the range of prying eyes. That's also why I insisted on handling all my own accounting records at the office. Delegating any financial responsibility to staff was a recipe for being defrauded by the very employees you trusted.

My quarterly investment statement had arrived from my exclusive Ottawa bank and I examined it back in my apartment.

It had been an extremely profitable quarter for my investments. In fact the past several years had been stellar.

My personal advisor had brilliantly recommended that I get out of stocks in May of 2007 and then just as wisely urged me to jump back in when the markets were at their worst levels in March of 2009. Now the stock markets, especially in the USA, were frothing again in record territory.

Mr. G. Leduc, my advisor, was now proposing that I pull back out of stocks and park my funds in cash and certain corporate bonds.

He never revealed what the initial "G" stood for, but as far as I was concerned his first name must be "Genius".

My net worth was now over seven million bucks and the obvious question staggered me.

Why was I still working?

Any nagging fears I might have harbored about my financial future were banished by the sheer bulk of my current wealth.

There was an enormous surplus already, vastly more than I could ever hope to spend, especially given my penchant for bargains and frugal living.

I called Corbett to let him know I was back.

Jim was pleased to hear from me and persuaded me to come over after supper for a visit.

For the rest of the afternoon I went downstairs to my office, looked over some recent files, and contemplated my future. Later I made myself a toasted peanut butter sandwich for supper.

The concept of a multi-millionaire eating such a basic Easter dinner struck me as bizarre.

When I arrived at Corbett's condo and had fetched myself a beer out of his refrigerator, I sat down and joked, "I met your clone in Las Vegas, a Catholic priest from Texas who is far too kind for his own good."

"How did you ever come into contact with a priest?" Jim teased.

I proceeded to tell Jim about meeting Timothy in the Houston airport and how he had squandered his meager life savings a day earlier to prevent some deadbeat family from getting evicted.

"That's just the sort of stupid move you would have made, Patsy."

"I like the sounds of him already," Jim answered. "I guess I can even overlook his profession."

Corbett hated religion. His parents had been fanatic Baptists and rammed their religious views down his throat throughout his entire childhood. He hadn't been to church except to attend funerals since he left home to begin university.

I continued relating the details of my trip, including sharing the room with Father Tim for the first week and with an old lady for the one Saturday night.

Corbett pressed me to explain how I had met Beatrice.

At first I was reluctant to tell him but he hounded me on the matter so I told him the whole story.

"Have aliens invaded your body, Slimy? In the forty odd years I've known you, this is the first time you've ever done anything altruistic. I'm shocked but extremely proud of you. You spent your whole vacation helping others. I'd sure like to meet that priest. It sounds like he's turned you into a human being."

"That's not the only piece of surprising news," I retorted. "I think I've decided this afternoon that I'm going to retire."

Jim was absolutely floored.

"I always figured you'd keep working until you dropped. What made you suddenly decide to pack it in?"

"I can't say for sure. For one thing, my quarterly investment statement from my financial advisor arrived while I was away, and I was stunned to realize how much I'm worth now. There's no point in accumulating any more money."

"I wholeheartedly agree with that, Boyd, especially since I'm fully aware of what a cheap bastard you are. You could easily survive on just the Old Age Pension the way you pinch pennies. Are you sure there isn't something else? You didn't get terrible news from your doctor, did you?"

Jim had a very concerned expression on his face when he broached the subject of my health, but I decided to be flippant anyway.

"Since I haven't even been to see a doctor in ten or fifteen years, I've got no idea what if anything might be wrong with me."

"I'm glad to hear that. There must be something besides money that prompted this sudden decision."

"It may have something to do with having lived with the priest for the week."

"Why do you say that?" Jim queried.

"We had some pretty intense discussions about our respective careers. His dedication to his parishioners was very impressive whereas I had to admit to myself that I just saw my own clients as cash cows. We talked in some depth about whether I was a crooked lawyer, and the answer wasn't clear. I have been taking advantage of little old ladies for a lot of years, and all for personal gain. I guess I may have been putting my own interests ahead of what was in my clients' best interests. Only I can properly judge that, but I do feel uncomfortable about some of my conduct."

"I'm stunned to hear you admit any of this," Jim interjected.

"This afternoon I examined a few of my more recent closed-out estate files. Even though I handled the matters quickly and efficiently, I noticed several things that I could have done differently. In each of those instances, I chose the option which put more money in my pocket. Suddenly I was looking at myself with new and critical eyes and I concluded that the best way to put an end to my predatory ways was to stop being a lawyer."

Corbett was fascinated with this line of thought and insisted on hearing the details regarding the files on which I now believed I had needlessly enriched myself.

I finally left his place at eleven o'clock and walked back home.

Despite the fact that the income from my investments earned me enough in ten minutes to pay for a cab ride, I was too thrifty to spring for a taxi.

That simply pounded home my conclusion that I had far more money than I would ever need.

CHAPTER 17 (Priestly Concerns)

Father Timothy was full of frustration after he got what seemed like a brush-off from the diocesan office.

What good was an appointment five months down the road? It seemed clear that the mental health of a poor priest in a poverty-stricken parish was not a priority with his superiors.

Over the ensuing week he waited for the return call from the Archbishop but it never came.

Timothy put it down to the hectic Holy Week which was by far the busiest period in the Catholic Church.

On Monday morning he called the diocesan office again but received only another runaround.

Resentment and despondency overtook Timothy that afternoon as he struggled with an old lawnmower to cut the rather tall grass around the church and rectory building.

How was doing that mundane task supposed to further the glory of God?

It took almost three hours to complete the job and Timothy was exhausted. He then showered and hauled his tired body off to the hospital in Jasper to make the visitation rounds.

Late that evening Timothy came to a monumental decision.

He would no longer allow himself to be used as a doormat. It was time to raise his concerns in a more public forum.

The priest tried to verbalize his confused thoughts in bed before he drifted off to sleep.

On Tuesday morning Timothy sat down on the church computer and began composing an article for the diocesan Catholic newspaper.

For the next three days he modified and amended the piece until he was satisfied that it accurately reflected his grave concerns.

He printed off a copy of the final draft and examined it.

*IS MY CATHOLIC CHURCH JUST ANOTHER MULTINATIONAL CORPORATION?*

*I'm a sixty-four year old Catholic priest, poor as a church mouse and recently plagued with self-doubts about my chosen vocation.*

*I've just begun my fortieth year in the priesthood. Did you realize that it took nine years of intensive university education before I could be ordained? I've been trained to be kind, wise and loyal to God's will and to my Catholic Church.*

*Recently I returned from my first vacation in many, many years, a one-week excursion to Las Vegas.*

*On the day before I was to leave, one of my parish families found themselves in threat of immediate eviction. I used $1,200 from my trip money to save them. I had no other savings so I left on my trip with only $230 to spend and no hotel accommodation arranged. My airline ticket was non-refundable so I flew off anyway knowing that I had grossly insufficient funds.*

*My church was unable to put me up for free in Las Vegas because a large Catholic retreat was taking place for visiting nuns and every available space was occupied.*

To compound the situation, the Las Vegas hotels were solidly booked and I found myself in a desperate situation.

Like the parable of the Good Samaritan, I was rescued by the most unlikely person, a wealthy but shady lawyer from Canada named Boyd. He permitted me to share his hotel room for the week and he paid for virtually all my other expenses.

God had certainly looked out for me.

In the course of my conversations with the lawyer, I piously suggested that Boyd was a crook, ripping off his elderly estate clients for vast personal gain.

He admitted that I was probably correct, but then he raised the most fascinating perspective.

Boyd declared that he and the Catholic Church were both in the business of milking widows.

I was angry and appalled by his blasphemy until he pointed out that he had prepared thousands of Wills for elderly clients and was uniquely aware of the pressure that all churches put on their faithful to be generous with both their donations and bequests.

Was this avaricious lawyer correct in his debasing assessment of my Catholic Church?

That wasn't the only controversial issue the attorney raised.

We had similar educations but he earned over $600,000 each year while my own salary is less than $20,000 including my car and apartment which is provided by the church.

Boyd didn't even need to work long hours to maintain his enormous income.

Disregard for a moment the requirement that I be perpetually on call in case of emergencies. I've calculated that for each of *the ninety hours I actually worked in a typical week, I received less than $5.*

*The lawyer pointed out that most other denominations pay their clergy salaries commensurate with their education and complex duties, but not my Catholic Church.*

*My lawyer friend insists that my Catholic Church is nothing but another greedy multinational corporation taking vile advantage of its employees.*

*The lawyer called me a slave.*
*Is he right about that as well?*

*Father Timothy Camacho,*
*Bleakwood, Texas*

Timothy was finally satisfied. Overcoming a brief temptation to delete the article and forget about the whole matter, he E-mailed it to the Catholic newspaper for the diocese of Lufkin and then sent a copy to Boyd Billingsworth.

Response was quick and decisive.

Archbishop Murphy telephoned Timothy in a rage the very next afternoon. The newspaper had contacted the Archbishop about the rebellious letter.

"I've ordered that your ill-considered whine be discarded, Father Camacho. I don't believe that I've ever seen such a wrong-headed interpretation of my beloved church. Have you been to see the diocesan counselor yet about your personal problems?"

"No, Archbishop. They can't fit me in until September. I was hoping to see you as soon as possible to discuss these matters and in fact I left two separate messages for you."

"This is the worst possible time for me because of all the evaluations and financial

meetings required at each parish. Your issues
need to be resolved with proper professionals.
I'll see if I can get them to move up your
appointment. In the meantime, please keep your
doubts to yourself. That's an order. No good
can come out of airing our dirty laundry in
public. Good day, Father."

Timothy felt utterly impotent and
abandoned.

CHAPTER 18 (Packing It in)

On Easter Sunday night I had a vivid and bizarre dream.

I was on trial for fraud. The Judge was up on the bench but hidden behind some type of waterfall which acted as a veil.

The prosecuting attorney on my right side was wearing an expensive black suit but there were horns protruding from the sides of his head.

Beside him were half a dozen demons, all dressed in black and also sporting horns. It was apparent that they formed part of his crack legal team.

Behind them was a large sign bearing the words "WITNESSES FOR THE PROSECUTION", and lined up under the sign were dozens of little old ladies. The line continued right out the courtroom door.

It must have been a closed courtroom because the public benches were empty except for one person sitting directly behind me.

I swung my head around to get a closer look at the audience of one.

It was the panhandler from Vegas with the orange Jesus shirt and he was frantically taking notes as if he were racing to make a deadline. He was still wearing that second orange shirt proclaiming "JESUS STILL LOVES YOU".

His presence offended me and I sarcastically said, "I see you finally got yourself a job."

He looked up, genuinely startled. I guess he hadn't been aware that I was watching him.

"Shouldn't you be devoting all your attention to that vast array of disgruntled witnesses?" he replied sadly.

I didn't respond to his comment. Why was he present but not the fellow to whom I handed $210? This trial seemed to be rigged against me.

When I glanced over to my left, I saw that my own defense team was also assembled.

Jim Corbett was wearing an old, torn legal robe, the sleeves in tatters.

His two assistants were both felines. I recognized Little Grey, the cat from the motel in Ozona, Texas, and Fluffy, Jean Powers' irritating pet. Both creatures were dressed in miniature legal robes.

Suddenly a deep authoritative voice boomed out from behind the veil of water.

"Mr. Prosecutor, please call your first witness."

For the remainder of the dream, one old woman after another took the stand and related in minute detail how I had overcharged her estate for the work I performed.

I couldn't even specifically remember many of the women and was petrified wondering how I could possibly contradict their allegations without access to my estate files.

Corbett wasn't even listening to the proceedings. He was using one of the torn sleeves on his law robe to play with the two cats.

It was a pathetic scene and I awoke covered in sweat.

It was only four in the morning but there was no way I was risking being thrown back into that terrifying nightmare.

I got up, showered and dressed.

An hour later I was downstairs in my office assessing my current files.

There were only twelve Wills in which I was the sole Estate Trustee, and another seven where I shared those duties with a close relative of the testatrix.

Of those nineteen files, five of the Wills were now under estate administration because the old dears had recently passed away. I found it odd that not a single one of my clients was male. I guess I really did specialize in milking widows and spinsters. My joke business cards were frighteningly accurate.

No new Wills were currently in the process of being prepared. Jean Powers had been the only pending file and I had managed to get her all signed up just before I left on my vacation.

With that awful dream still fresh in my mind, I decided to be generous with these final clients and give each of them a substantial break on my legal fees.

By doing that, if I got thrown back into that awful dream, perhaps at least I could muster up a few satisfied clients to counter the legion of disgruntled ones.

Easter Monday was never a holiday in my office, so by the time Florence arrived for work at nine o'clock, I was beginning to get a handle on each of my current files. I asked her to come in to my office.

"Florence, I had a really great time in Las Vegas and gave my career a lot of deep thought. As of today we're not accepting any new clients or new business. I'm going to wind down my law practice as expeditiously as possible."

"My goodness, Mr. Billingsworth, I'm shocked. Does this mean that I'll be out of job soon?"

"Eventually, but for now I'll still require your services as usual and I won't cut

your salary even if gradually the hours I
require you here diminish."

We chatted for a few minutes about what
had gone on in the office during my absence
and I signed some correspondence and gave her
some instructions regarding a few ongoing
files.

Later I perused a list of the Wills I had
in safekeeping. There were hundreds of them.
In my greedy quest for future income, I had
urged my clients to leave their original Wills
with me, heeding the traditional legal wisdom
that I'd have a much greater chance of scoring
the moderately lucrative estate legal work if
I retained possession of the original Will.

Now I was suddenly motivated to dump those
Wills back to the clients or hand them off to
another lawyer.

I pored through the yellow pages of the
Belleville phone book trying to analyze which
lawyer might be a good prospect to take over
my files.

One tiny advertisement caught my eye.

Three younger female attorneys had
recently joined forces and their ad indicated
that they handled Wills and Estates. Their
offices were in some sort of shared set-up
downtown in which many struggling lawyers were
attempting to keep overhead at a minimum while
still giving the illusion of having a proper
office.

Florence had explained the arrangement to
me several months earlier when I happened to
ask her if she knew why so many lawyers had
that same office address.

I phoned their office and was pleased to
discover that they too were working on Easter
Monday. I arranged to treat them to supper at

a fancy steakhouse just a few doors down from their office.

After introductions were made and we had placed our food orders, I began by asking them questions about their partnership and business.

"At the moment we're just treading water," the one named Amanda admitted. "New clients are hard to come by, but we're managing to pay our bills with duty counsel and legal aid work."

"How are you faring with the Wills and Estates portion of your law practice?" I asked.

"Not well," the second young lady named Martina replied. "It's not easy prying clients away from their current lawyer. I'm certainly hoping that changes soon because I really prefer the office work. I don't feel comfortable in court even handling the minor matters I normally get at this early stage of my career."

The third lady was named Rita, and she was a bit older, perhaps in her early thirties. She was the only one I had previously met at some law function a year or two earlier.

Over the next hour I listened as they talked about their views on being a lawyer. All three impressed me as good, honest practitioners.

"I've just decided to retire," I announced, "and I might be interested in letting you take over my law practice, even rent space in my office building if that suited your needs. Would you be agreeable to taking a look at my operation later this week?"

"Unfortunately we're all broke," Rita answered. "We'd love the opportunity to get some immediate new clients but we don't have two cents to rub together."

"Believe it or not, I wouldn't require any compensation from you. I'm quite well to do. What I am looking for is someone who will look after my rather elderly client base and perhaps take over my role as Estate Trustee in those instances in which the clients are willing to transfer responsibility."

That proposal was met with great relish by the ladies, who agreed to come over to my office the following afternoon to discuss the matter further.

That night the disturbing dream continued with a constant parade of angry dead clients. This time around I did remember most of them and I was shocked at the intricate legal knowledge that each of them now possessed. They testified word for word what I had assured them before they died, and then pointed out how my actual representation of their estates blatantly broke those solemn promises.

When I woke up the next morning I felt ashamed and sleazy.

The three female lawyers arrived at three o'clock as agreed. I asked them how much income they were currently earning.

They hadn't been kidding when they said that they were scrambling just to make ends meet. None of them had made more than $8,000 in the past year, not even Rita.

It surprised me how difficult it was for other attorneys to make big bucks. Greedy scoundrels like me thrived while honest conscientious lawyers struggled. What a perverse society we live in!

I showed the ladies around and said that I would put together a proposal and run it by them at my office on Thursday afternoon.

I had already decided that I was comfortable passing my clients over to these young lawyers. I had contacted a few of my colleagues plus a couple of judges, and everyone who had dealt with the ladies had found them courteous, competent and honorable.

On Wednesday I met with a chartered accountant in order to ascertain the tax implications of closing up or transferring my law practice. I had more than two million bucks sitting in my professional corporation and the accountant made recommendations as to how I could lessen my income tax burden.

I woke up on Thursday morning relieved that for the second night in a row I hadn't been plagued by that disturbing nightmare.

The girls arrived late in the afternoon and I showed them around the building.

Inside the main front door there was a spacious foyer with a staircase in the center leading upstairs to my apartment.

On the left side of the staircase was the door to my office and on the right side was another door behind which were three rooms that I was presently using just for storage. That was the area I was offering to the ladies and they were impressed with the size and layout of the space.

We sat down in my office and I made my presentation.

"Now that I've decided to retire, I'm quite antsy about wrapping up my legal practice quickly. How much do you pay right now for your office space?"

Rita answered, "It costs us $600 per month plus another $800 for the use of the equipment and a shared receptionist."

"Is that arrangement working out well for you?"

"Not really," Amanda replied. "There are too many lawyers sharing use of the copier, the fax and the main desktop computers."

"Do you own any office equipment yourselves?" I queried.

"We each have our own laptop computers and our Blackberry devices, but that's all," Martina responded.

"If you're interested in moving here, I'd be willing to rent you the space I'm not using for $400 per month and I'll give you some useable office equipment. In addition, to get you started on the right foot, I'll pay each of you $5,000 each month which will entitle me to twenty-five hours of your time to assist me in wrapping up my business."

The ladies appeared stunned.

"Think about it," I continued. "I don't want to rush you, but if you determine that my offer doesn't meet your needs, then I'll have to find someone else quickly. I've got too many elderly clients relying on me that I can't just close up and walk away from my practice. I feel an obligation to provide them with some continuity and not abandon them."

"May we discuss your proposal in private for a few minutes, Mr. Billingsworth?" Rita asked. "We may be able to give you an answer this afternoon."

They adjourned back to the office space I had offered them and I waited in my office.

Twenty minutes later they returned and indicated that they would be thrilled to accept my most generous offer and would like to commence the arrangement on May 1$^{st}$ which was next Thursday.

I accepted, shook their hands and welcomed them to 210 Church Street.

I wrote a check payable to their law firm for $15,000 to cover the first month of their time, and I've never seen three happier faces as they thanked me and rushed down to their bank to deposit the funds.

It was definitely a win-win situation. I was now committed to retirement and had three fine young attorneys to assume whichever of my clients opted to continue with them. My three new colleagues suddenly found themselves with a decent income and I had put a bit of the money stuck in my professional corporation to work assisting these women with bettering their legal careers.

On Saturday I hired a young fellow who had a tiny apartment in the old Boyle building next door, and we moved everything out of the ladies' space. Most of the files we lugged upstairs to an empty room. We also moved some spare office equipment and furniture into the space, some of which I had been storing upstairs and the rest of which had been collecting dust in the dingy basement.

It took us all day and I paid the kid a nice bonus.

That evening I walked over to Corbett's condo and brought him up-to-date about these new arrangements.

"Just like I said before, Slimy, aliens have definitely taken over your body. Did you visit Area 51 when you were in Las Vegas? There's no way the Boyd Billingsworth I've known for forty years would ever show generosity, especially to a competitor. What's gotten into you?"

"Don't ask me to explain it, Jim. It must be the time I spent with the priest. Somehow that experience opened my eyes and I was able to look at how I've been running my business through new lenses. I actually believe that I'm growing a conscience because I've had some disturbing dreams lately and you're in them."

Jim insisted that I tell him about the nightmares, which he found most amusing.

As I was about to leave, Corbett made a fascinating observation.

"Spending time with the priest definitely changed you for the better, Slimy. For the priest's sake, I hope spending a week with a scuzzy lawyer hasn't poisoned his outlook on life."

CHAPTER 19 (Another Roommate)

On Sunday morning I attended the service at the United Church next door to my building.

For once I wasn't there to attract new clients but instead wanted to really listen to the sermon.

Unfortunately I got nothing out of the service and decided that religion was a complete waste of time for me.

Any faith I once had was extinguished when Gabriela got sick and withered away with the cancer. Trying to rekindle the spark now was futile. Religion obviously wasn't my cup of tea. Perhaps I was too cynical to comprehend the message or maybe I was simply not gullible enough to take the bait offered by the clergy.

Just before supper my apartment phone rang. It was the hospital advising me that Jean Powers had been brought in that morning after suffering a stroke. She was somewhat stabilized now but was beside herself with worry about her cat and had begged the nurse to contact me.

I agreed to come over to the hospital immediately in order to get Jean's house key and then go feed Fluffy.

I wasn't thrilled about the prospect of temporarily looking after the annoying little weasel, but I had specifically promised Jean that I'd care for her cat if and when needed.

My recent dreams flashed in my mind as I recalled the extensive line-up of angry old clients who believed that I had broken my promises to them.

Old Jean Powers weakly squeezed my hand as she handed me her house key.

"The doctor says that I'll have to stay in hospital for at least a few weeks, Mr.

Billingsworth. Fluffy shouldn't be left alone at night. He's almost twenty years old. Is there anything you can do?"

"Of course, Jean; I'll go get Fluffy now and he can keep me company in my apartment until you're able to get back into your home. Don't worry about a thing. Old Fluffy will be just fine. Now please get some rest. Everything will work out for you and Fluffy."

"You're an angel, Mr. Billingsworth. I knew from the minute I met you in church that you could be trusted."

I drove over to Queen Street and parked in Jean's driveway. Fluffy came limping over to me as soon as he heard the key in the lock and he immediately began rubbing up against my leg while purring loudly.

The cat food was in the kitchen cupboard where Jean had told me it was, so I carried a couple of bags of the hard cat food and several assorted tins of the soft food to the front hall.

I scouted around and located a cat cage in the basement and the kitty litter tray in a small room off the kitchen.

Since I was also Jean's Power of Attorney, I checked her refrigerator and confiscated or discarded any food that might spoil.

I loaded the cat's food and litter box into the trunk of my car and then eased Fluffy into the cat carrier.

Back in my apartment I fed Fluffy and let him explore the place.

The little bugger followed me around constantly. When I sat on the couch to watch TV, Fluffy immediately struggled up onto my lap and stayed there.

Every time I had to get up for another beer or to go to the bathroom, Fluffy would follow me and then climb back up on my lap.

Surprisingly I didn't mind the attention. I was dressed in casual clothes so his constantly shedding cat hair didn't bother me this time around.

Fluffy snuggled up to me in bed and I fell asleep to the soft sound of his gentle purring. That comforting hum made me realize that I didn't hate cats after all.

On Monday morning Amanda phoned first thing to ask if I'd mind them moving their files and other office possessions over to their new space today instead of Wednesday. They had found another lawyer willing to take over their existing space if and only if they could vacate immediately. The girls were pleased because it meant they wouldn't have to give any notice or pay the May rental costs.

"Certainly, Amanda; on the weekend I had a young neighbor assist me in moving all my stuff out of your space, so everything's all ready for you. I even rounded up some spare office furniture and equipment for you."

Florence arrived at nine o'clock and I let her know that the three women attorneys would be moving in later in the day. I could sense that she was wondering how all these changes would affect her.

Fluffy had meowed pitifully when I went to leave my apartment this morning so I let him wander downstairs since I had no appointments booked.

I introduced Florence to my new furry roommate. She looked at me like I was demented but said nothing.

Monday and Tuesday were both hectic days around 210 Church Street.

The lady lawyers moved their few office belongings and files into their new space and were delighted with the furniture and equipment I had provided.

I drove over to Jean's house around noon on Monday and carried back three cat baskets I had noticed there. I put one of them in my office near my desk so Fluffy could nap comfortably while I worked.

On Monday evening I went back to the hospital to visit Jean and assured her that Fluffy and I had bonded already and that he had slept on the bed with me.

I could tell how utterly relieved she was to hear that her beloved pet was happy.

Again as I left she held my hand and told me that I was Fluffy's guardian angel and that she felt at peace.

Jean looked extremely frail.

On the way out I had a brief chat with the doctor on duty. He said that Jean had already developed serious complications from the stroke and that her condition was quite precarious.

His evaluation turned out to be quite astute because Jean died in her sleep very early on Tuesday morning.

My new legal tenants had their telephone hooked up on Tuesday morning and were ready for business by noon.

That afternoon I asked Martina if she had a few minutes to discuss an estate matter with me.

"An elderly client of mine just passed away this morning and I'm her sole Estate Trustee. Would you be willing to handle the legal work on the estate?"

"Oh, yes, I'd be pleased to do so. Thank you so much for the business, Mr. Billingsworth."

"Have you handled any estates before?" I inquired.

"No, I haven't," Martina replied. "This will be my very first estate although I have prepared a few Wills."

"That's fine; I'll be able to teach you exactly what has to be done so you'll be almost an expert by the time this estate gets wrapped up."

For the next hour I went over in detail with Martina what my initial duties were as Estate Trustee and what Martina would need to do as soon as I had completed the preliminary inventory of Jean's assets.

Later that afternoon I confirmed the funeral arrangements with the funeral home. Later I brought Martina over to Jean's house so that we could search together through her possessions looking for financial information and ensuring that no cash or other valuables were lying around the house.

Friday, May 2$^{nd}$ was taken up with Jean's small funeral, attended by about twenty friends and neighbors. Jean had no close relatives and all her estate was bequeathed to various charities including her church.

That evening I checked my personal E-mails on my apartment computer and read Father Tim's article.

I replied, "What have we done to each other? As soon as I got back home I decided to retire and stop gouging my clients. In just a few days I've persuaded three honest young female attorneys to set up shop in my building and I'm referring all new business over to them. My days as a slimy, greedy shyster have come to an end. My buddy Corbett blames you. He says either a week in your presence has redeemed me or aliens have taken over my body. Now I find that you've morphed into a radical priest who dares to question the ancient wisdom of the Catholic Church. Please tell me I haven't corrupted you. Keep in touch and keep your hands out of the collection plate."

CHAPTER 20 (Defiance, Rebellion, Consequences)


Father Timothy got a kick out of Boyd's E-mail response when he read it.

For the next week Timothy worked incessantly with a host of home and hospital visits as well as the normal maintenance of the church and grounds. Each workday was long and tiring.

It galled him that the Archbishop had censored the diocesan newspaper article. Deep doubts like Timothy was wrestling with shouldn't be ignored.

He continued to seethe about the whole situation until it was time to prepare for the Saturday late afternoon mass on May 4$^{th}$.

Timothy strayed off the assigned topic and instead used his homily to attack the scourge of businesses striving to maximize profits at the expense of fairness to their employees.

After the service Timothy spotted Douglas Grant, the editor of the local weekly community newspaper, who was lingering in the church parking lot chatting with a friend.

When Grant was about to climb into his car, Timothy walked over and asked if Doug had a moment to peruse an article, and the priest handed his censored lament to the newspaperman.

When Grant had read it, he remarked "Wow, this is fascinating, Father Tim. Can I publish it in our next edition?"

"I'm conflicted about it, Doug. My Archbishop has ordered me not to make my doubts public and he wouldn't allow my article to be published in our diocesan paper. You're a good Catholic. Should I keep my concerns to myself?"

"My gut instinct as an editor is to encourage you to let me publish the piece. I've never evaluated our church in the way your lawyer friend does. Do you really feel oppressed?"

"I've been lonely and exhausted for a long time, but until those discussions with the attorney, the idea that the church was purposely taking advantage of me never crossed my mind. Now I can't seem to think about anything else and I'm beginning to conclude that the lawyer may be correct."

"Will you get in any trouble if the article is published?"

"It's highly probable but I have no idea what the precise consequences might be. I've been an obedient priest for thirty-nine years. That has to count for something. Likely I'll just receive a stern reprimand."

"It seems to me, Father Tim, that by raising these issues, you'd be speaking up for every other priest out there who may have the same doubts but is afraid to rock the boat. It's probably an issue that only a veteran priest can fully understand and have the courage to question. It's your call."

Timothy mulled it over for a moment and then said, "Go ahead and publish it. I'm not comfortable with the Archbishop ordering me to shut up, and I'll accept whatever happens to me."

"I congratulate you for your bravery, Father Tim. In fact, I'll head over to the newspaper office right now and submit it. Our deadline is later this evening so your article will appear in the next edition which will be printed up tomorrow and distributed on Monday."

"I certainly hope that the blowback on me isn't too harsh," Timothy joked. "Occasionally in the past I've felt that the church was structured a lot like the military, and I'd hate to get severely punished for this first instance of mild insubordination."

Timothy spent the rest of Saturday evening amending his Sunday homily. His new message for tomorrow's holy masses was entitled "SPEAKING YOUR MIND".

Before he went to bed, Timothy went down to the rectory office and E-mailed to Boyd Billingsworth the webpage address of the community newspaper and advised his lawyer friend that the article would be published in Monday's edition despite the fact that the Archbishop had forbidden Tim from airing his beefs in public.

When Timothy returned to the church on Monday afternoon after several hours of visitations, there were eleven messages on the rectory answering machine.

Three of them were from the diocesan office in Lufkin. One was from a fellow priest and the remaining calls were from parishioners who made surprisingly negative comments about the article.

Controversial news certainly travelled fast.

Only the priest and the diocesan office had wanted Timothy to return their calls, so Timothy first called Father Juan Rodrigues from the neighboring parish of Newton. Father Juan was much younger than Timothy and had only been a priest for five years.

Timothy was astonished at the outrage voiced by Father Juan who called Tim an ungrateful traitor and a blasphemer. Timothy tried to remain polite but when Father Juan's tirade became abusive, Timothy fired back.

"I don't believe you appreciated the points I was making, Father Juan. You're young and haven't reached the burnout stage of your career, but I assure you it will come. The solitude eventually becomes unbearable. There are other serious issues that I didn't raise but which need to be addressed. I have come to gravely question some of our church's basic doctrines. We should be permitted to marry and live normal family lives. This celibate lifestyle we're forced to endure is entirely unnatural, and it has turned me in to something very closely resembling an alcoholic. Women should be fully equal to men and should be allowed into the priesthood. That change alone would overcome the dire shortage of priests which currently forces us to work such long and burdensome hours. Please don't dismiss everything I raised in the newspaper without first giving the matters your deepest contemplation."

Father Juan bellowed, "Absolute nonsense!" and slammed the receiver down on Timothy.

His next call was to the Archbishop's office. Father Bruce came on the line first and berated Timothy for disregarding a direct order from the Archbishop.

Then the executive assistant threatened Timothy.

"Before I put you through to His Holiness, let me remind you that your pension can be withdrawn at the sole discretion of the church. Whatever the Archbishop instructs you to do to mitigate the damage you've caused, you'd better damn well comply."

The Archbishop himself was beyond angry and tore a strip off Timothy for a full five minutes. He accepted his reprimand in deferential silence even though he deplored the tone of superior dismissal evident in the Archbishop's strident voice.

"Father Bruce and I have discussed how your flagrant attack on our church can be overcome, and we have decided that you must write a follow-up letter, the content of which must be fully approved by me. In your sincere apology you will divulge your personal demons and ask the Catholic Church for forgiveness. You must totally recant the obscene charges that you have leveled at our church and explain that one brief moment of weakness and loneliness induced by alcohol had caused you to momentarily lose your sense of perspective. Father Bruce has already drafted an appropriate letter for you to sign."

By now Timothy had had just about enough of his pious cohorts. He was being treated like a petulant child and his genuine concerns were being swept under the rug like so much irrelevant and unwanted dust. A rebellion welled up inside him and he decided to stand his ground.

"I'm sorry, Archbishop Murphy, but I refuse. The issues of overwork, insufficient remuneration and the dreadful solitude faced by priests like me in our church must be addressed. The article I gave to the paper is the beginning of the discussion, not the end. Feel free to have Father Bruce compose his own letter to the editor rebutting my article. I have no intention of signing any letter I don't believe is true."

"How dare you ignore my direct orders and mock our sincere attempts to minimize the damage your disgusting outburst has caused. We have ways of coercing your cooperation."

"Your Holiness, do you not believe that dialogue about these issues is far superior than burying them through the use of vague and insulting threats?"

Timothy immediately regretted such a cheeky response, but the words had already poured out of his lips.

The Archbishop's reaction was furious indignation.

"That does it, Father Camacho," he screeched. "As of this very minute I am relieving you of all your priestly duties. My office will make arrangements to have another priest or a deacon take over immediate responsibility for your parish. You are forbidden to use the church vehicle, the telephone or the computer. Please ensure that you have removed yourself and all your belongings from the rectory quarters by Friday afternoon."

Timothy realized that he had pushed too far but this heavy-handed response was shocking. How could he possibly survive? He was completely dependent on the goodwill of the church.

"Will I continue to be paid by the diocese? At the moment my life savings are less than $1,200."

"No, you will certainly not continue to be paid. You are no longer in the employ of this diocese or the Catholic Church. Father Bruce will calculate how much you are owed for your work up until today, and he will deposit those funds into your bank account. By the way, this asinine little rebellion has just cost you any church pension that you might have been granted from the retired priests' fund. Those payments are absolutely discretionary as you are no doubt fully aware. The pension fund is also unregistered and thereby fully exempt from state and federal laws. Now, before I set these punitive matters in motion, this is your last opportunity to repent and toe the line. Have I persuaded you to comply with my requirements in order to retain your job and all the generous benefits that come with it?"

Timothy wasn't even the least bit tempted to cave in now. Surely God would look after him. Timothy's faith was unshaken. It was just his new attitude about the Catholic Church that was causing all this internal commotion. He let the Archbishop have it with both barrels.

"On the contrary, Archbishop Murphy, your reaction disgusts me and reinforces my suspicions that my lawyer friend was right. The Catholic Church is an abusive employer. This scurrilous attempt to coerce my obedience through intimidation borders on the downright evil. You've picked the wrong priest to bully."

For the second time in less than an hour Father Timothy heard the sound of a telephone receiver being slammed down in his ear.

Timothy was totally benumbed by these abrupt developments. In the space of a few minutes he had lost his job, his pension, use of the car, and he was being unceremoniously evicted from his living quarters in the rectory.

At the ripe old age of sixty-four, Timothy was on the verge of being homeless and virtually penniless.

That was certainly a result infinitely more disastrous than the severe reprimand Timothy had fully expected to receive.

There was only one thing the priest could do at this moment to alleviate his shock.

He cracked open one beer and then another and another.

For supper he cooked frozen fish and chips. The food in his refrigerator belonged to him and now he had just three days to use up anything frozen or perishable.

Father Tim went to bed thoroughly intoxicated at half past nine.

CHAPTER 21 (Get Out NOW)

On Tuesday morning just after nine o'clock, Timothy saw Deacon Maurice Enright drive up to the rectory and enter.

Since Timothy was in the process of eating a huge portion of bacon and eggs for breakfast, he stayed up in his living quarters.

About an hour later the elderly deacon rapped softly on Timothy's door and requested that he come downstairs for a moment.

The deacon handed Timothy a piece of paper and said, "This fax just came in for you, addressed to the attention of both of us."

Tim began reading.

It was a formal confirmation of all the dire consequences the Archbishop had enunciated, with the additional insult of demanding the return of all priestly garments and other property of the church including the parish credit card.

Timothy's final severance was simply his regular pay for the period from the 1$^{st}$ of May until yesterday, and the fax confirmed that this sum had now been duly deposited into his bank account.

The faxed letter brazenly stated that the Catholic Church had now fully met all its legal obligations toward Timothy and that their mutual association was hereby formally terminated.

The final insulting paragraph put forward the suggestion that Timothy should seek to be "laicized" so that the church would be spared the expense of proceeding with his formal "defrocking" which was clearly justified because of Timothy's blatant heresy.

As Timothy stood up to leave, the deacon hesitantly advised that, "Father Bruce phoned earlier just after he sent the fax. The diocese prefers that you vacate your living quarters immediately rather than on Friday, and they will secure a ride for you across the state line to DeRidder, Louisiana where the church will pay for your motel room for the next three nights."

"My bank is in Jasper, Moe. Will the diocese put me up there instead?"

"I'll call Father Bruce in Lufkin about that and get back to you shortly."

Timothy headed upstairs to begin packing his clothes, personal items and useable food.

The deacon entered the apartment a few minutes later.

"I'm sorry, Father Tim, but the Archbishop wants you out of the parish and out of Texas. The motel offer is only good for DeRidder but the ride they've arranged will drive you to Jasper first so that you can do your banking. Please don't be angry with me, Father, but I've been ordered to monitor your packing to ensure that no church property is removed."

Tim was deeply insulted but agreed to these new terms.

The ride arrived at one o'clock and Timothy loaded his suitcase, sports bag and two cardboard boxes into the van.

Petulantly he had insisted that Deacon Enright write out and sign a letter confirming that no church property had been taken. Tim handed in the credit card and his keys but kept one priest's outfit which belonged to him personally. His mother had given it to Tim one year as a Christmas gift a few months before she had died.

It dawned on Timothy that he was being treated in exactly the same manner as a fired employee of a large company, escorted abruptly off the premises carrying his personal belongings.

The chap who drove the van was very accommodating and waited patiently while Tim cleaned out all but $39 from his bank account in Jasper, which sum symbolically represented a dollar for each full year of faithful service the priest had given to the Catholic Church.

On the short drive across the state border to DeRidder, the driver chatted amiably about retirement and then waited to ensure that the church had made satisfactory arrangements with the modest motel before he headed back to Texas.

Timothy was well and truly abandoned and alone now.

He unpacked a few clothes and took the beer he had salvaged from his refrigerator out of the cardboard box. He retrieved some ice from a machine in the motel lobby, put a few cans on ice to chill, and walked in to the small town to purchase a phone card.

Timothy's initial plan was to have a celebratory supper in town, but with money worries now beginning to engulf him, he opted instead to eat bread, crackers and chips out of one of the boxes.

As he sipped beer afterwards, Timothy chastised himself for telling the Archbishop that he had picked the wrong priest to bully. Not only had it been a childish comment, but Timothy was obviously the ideal candidate for abuse. He had no influential friends, no financial resources, no relatives and in fact nowhere to go.

Tim's parents had died many years earlier and he had been an only child.

He now regretted having urged his dear mother, who had died a year after his father, to give all of her very modest estate to the Catholic Church. At the time Timothy believed that he had no use for money, knowing that his beloved church would always look after him.

Timothy broke out laughing as he recalled a famous Sarah Palin comeback line.

"How's that working out for you?"

At least Timothy did have a small income to anticipate in a few months. He would turn sixty-five in September and could apply for his government social security. It wouldn't provide much but nevertheless it would come in mighty handy.

Timothy wondered if he could even find a job. The Catholic Church certainly wouldn't be providing any letters of reference.

Perhaps the Lord would provide for Timothy like He had done in Las Vegas.

Timothy prayed for wisdom and a few minutes later decided it would be wise to crack open a beer.

Harsh reality suddenly hit home. Not only was Timothy soon to be homeless, but he had no idea even where to have his mail forwarded. Depression and panic were lurking in the depths of his mind when Timothy finally drifted off to sleep.

The following morning Timothy awoke surprisingly refreshed. The day was sunny and full of promise.

His first call using his new phone card was to Douglas Grant, the editor of the community newspaper.

"Hello, Doug; it's Timothy Camacho."

"Hi, Father Tim; have you had much response about your article?"

"I certainly have. First off, I'm no longer Father Timothy. The Archbishop has already relieved me of all my priestly duties and evicted me from the rectory quarters. The church has paid for a motel room in DeRidder for three nights to get rid of me immediately, and I've lost my church pension and no longer draw a salary from the church."

"That's dreadful! Perhaps that explains the conversations I had with Deacon Enright and with a Father Bruce from the diocesan office in Lufkin. They didn't mention that you had been let go but they did implore me not to publish any follow-up piece or any letters commenting on your article."

"If you choose to disobey their request, Doug, it does seem quite newsworthy how they've mistreated me. You certainly have my permission to interview me and publish another story on this new development."

"I'm so sorry, Father Tim, but we're a community newspaper and our owner has ordered me to bury all responses. I'm afraid that the rest of your story is going to remain unheard unless you're able to convince another newspaper to run it."

"I understand. Just to satisfy my curiosity, have you received any feedback?"

"Yes, we've had many E-mails."

"Were they sympathetic to my concerns?"

"The ones from Catholics have been heavily critical of you, but the few from non-Catholics have tended to agree with your side of things. Normally I'd pursue an interesting situation like yours, but I can't disobey my boss. I've got a wife and kids to support and at my age I don't want to be looking for another job."

"I can't disagree with your logic, Doug. Thanks for running the piece in the first place. I told you that I'd accept whatever consequences arose and I guess that's what I'll have to do. A pipsqueak like me can't fight a powerful organization like the church."

For a combination breakfast and lunch, Timothy ate some bread with the rest of his cheese slices before they spoiled, and washed it all down with some warm Pepsi.

Then he laid out all his clothing and possessions on the bed and carpet.

If he was going to be a homeless drifter, then he needed to reduce the bulk of what he would need to carry around with him.

By repacking carefully Timothy managed to render the two cardboard boxes redundant so long as he ate the remaining food before he had to check out of the motel on Friday morning.

Minor problems like finding a forwarding address for his mail would just have to wait. At this precise point in time, Timothy couldn't care less what happened to his mail.

Supper consisted of the rest of the bread, chips and crackers, complemented with the remainder of the large bottle of Pepsi.

Since there were only three cans of beer left, Tim decided to save them for Thursday evening to celebrate the last night during which he had a guaranteed roof over his head.

Thursday brought rain so Tim stayed in the motel room all day and ate the bits and pieces of his remaining food.

Late in the evening after his third beer, Timothy had an epiphany.

He did have one solitary friend in this huge world, Boyd Billingsworth from Canada.

Timothy resolved to call his friend in the morning before he checked out of the motel.

Perhaps the lawyer would have some useful advice to dole out.

## CHAPTER 22 (Building Improvements)

I was able to obtain investment statements from Jean Powers' two banks, and got valuation opinions from three different realtors regarding the suggested listing price of Jean's lovely old home.

Two local dealers evaluated the jewelry, furniture and antiques, so by the following Thursday, May 8$^{th}$, I was able to provide Martina with the approximate value of Jean's estate so the young lawyer could prepare and submit the proper forms to the Surrogate Court.

I selected a realtor and listed the home even though nothing could be sold until the official Certificate of Appointment had been granted. Real estate closing dates normally take place a month or two after an Offer is accepted, so I felt it was prudent to list immediately. Expensive century homes are not always easy to dispose of.

I spent a lot of time with Martina each working day, educating her regarding the role of an estate lawyer and allowing her to take over the legal work on the other estates which were in the process of being wound up.

Most of the elderly living clients who had designated me as Power of Attorney and Estate Trustee were completely willing to turn those tasks over to Martina and either Amanda or Rita. As an added protection for the clients, I recommended naming two of the women lawyers and requiring both signatures to bind any action. The public would be shocked to learn how often a trusted individual lawyer, who is the only named Power of Attorney before death and the sole Estate Trustee after the person dies, winds up blatantly stealing the funds.

The lack of a second pair of eyes monitoring an attorney's conduct is a recipe for that lawyer succumbing to temptation and misappropriating the client's money.

In each case I set up a meeting in the client's home, introduced the ladies to the client, and explained that I was now a senior citizen myself and had finally decided to retire after toiling for forty years in the legal business.

As an incentive for the clients, I agreed to pay the legal cost of preparing the new documents whether or not that client opted to transfer responsibility over to Martina and her partners. I didn't want any clients feeling pressured into switching over to Martina's firm, but I was also anxious for each client to amend their Wills quickly and remove me as Estate Trustee.

That incentive worked wonders and I hoped to be free of every single estate trusteeship within another week or two. With any luck I could wrap up the bulk of my estate administration work and distribute the final funds to the applicable beneficiaries by the end of May, the only exception being Jean Powers' estate.

Complete freedom was definitely knocking on the door of my law office.

Since I was paying the three lawyers well, I used the services of Rita and Amanda to help Martina with the estate work, and Florence began working full days in order to receive a promised fat bonus.

Florence was invaluable in showing the young women in detail what was required in the way of paperwork on each file.

I had always prided myself on moving my estate administrations along quickly and efficiently, but with all hands now on deck, we were operating in overdrive.

On Friday morning my apartment telephone rang at eight o'clock in the morning, an extremely unusual occurrence.

I didn't recognize the caller's voice when he asked to speak with Boyd Billingsworth.

"This is Boyd speaking."

"Boyd, this is Tim Camacho phoning."

"It's great to hear from you, Father Timothy. I found your article on the internet. Are you everybody's hero now for speaking up?"

"Not exactly," he answered and then told me the horrible events that had swamped him because of the newspaper piece.

"I'm shocked!" I blurted out when he had finished. "What are you going to live on?"

"My life savings are only about $1,500, plus I'll begin collecting a bit of social security once I turn sixty-five in September," the priest admitted.

"Where will you live?"

"I'll be homeless as soon as I check out of the motel later this morning. I've got no relatives or friends. The Catholic Church has been my whole life. Strangely, though, I'm not depressed about this unexpected professional setback. In fact I feel a glorious sense of absolute freedom. I'm calling you now to let you know what's happened to me because there's no way you'll be able to reach me."

"I'm your friend, Tim. Why don't you come up here to Canada and stay with me for the time being? I'll wire you the plane fare. I'm just wrapping up my law practice which I hope to complete in another month or two. It'll be great to have some company to help me pass the time. Without realizing it, you've been

163

responsible for mammoth changes in my life and outlook."

"I'd love to come up to Canada for a visit. Thanks so much for the offer of a plane ticket, but I'll make my own way there. It's very comforting at this moment to know that I have a destination. With any luck I'll be there in a few days knocking on your door. You'll never know how much I appreciate this."

"I can't wait to discuss everything with you, Timothy. If you run into any difficulty on your way up here, just call me and I'll do whatever it takes to help you."

After I hung up I let Fluffy get back on my lap and said, "We're going to have a house guest, sweetie. I'll have to find another spot to put your kitty litter. We can't have our spare bedroom smelling like a toilet. Father Timothy has already been through enough shit."

I decided to treat myself to breakfast downtown.

As I walked outside it struck me how rundown my building looked. It had been almost twenty years since I had the bricks painted their current lime green, and the paint had peeled away in countless places exposing the original red bricks underneath.

Even I had to admit that the old building looked most unsightly.

When I returned to the office after breakfast, I phoned the company which had done the previous paint job. Tony, who still owned the business, came over immediately and gave me a quote. He indicated that he had a break in his work schedule and could do the job right away. I didn't even dicker over his price and by one o'clock his crew began removing the old lime green paint.

By Saturday afternoon they had finished the preparation work and began painting the bricks a reddish color very similar to the original bricks.

Jim Corbett had some sort of flu bug so we missed our weekly Saturday night beer fest at his condo.

That night I had another continuation of the bad dream, the first such nightmare in a couple of weeks.

The courtroom drama was continuing with prosecution witnesses, but the line of old ladies had shrunk. Finally the last one testified and the opposing lead lawyer announced in a deep, hissing voice, "The prosecution rests".

The Judge's booming voice penetrated the waterfall. "Does the defense intend to call any witnesses?"

Corbett stood up wearing the same tattered legal robe. Little Grey and Fluffy also rose up on their hind legs like tiny people.

"The accused is our one and only witness, Your Honor," Corbett replied.

"Boyd Billingsworth, take the stand," the Judge ordered.

I was more frightened than nervous, and fortunately I woke up at that point.

The crew finished painting the brickwork on Sunday morning and then they painted all the trim and window-sills a lovely deep pink.

By late afternoon the building was all tarted up with colors befitting a firm of up-and-coming female lawyers.

Fluffy was even more affectionate than usual on Sunday evening and seemed to crave my attention every second. The instant I stopped petting him, he would let out a plaintive meow. When I got into bed, Fluffy lay down on my pillow with his paw resting on my face. He was certainly a devoted companion. It was no wonder that old ladies adored their cats.

On Monday morning when I woke up, Fluffy hadn't even moved. I let him sleep in while I showered and dressed.

When Fluffy didn't emerge for breakfast, I went back in the bedroom to wake him up, but Fluffy had died in his sleep.

I guessed that his extra affection the previous evening had been his way of saying goodbye.

Cats must sense these things.

CHAPTER 23 (A Hitchhiking Adventure)

Shortly after calling Boyd Billingsworth, Timothy packed up his worldly possessions and checked out of the motel.

He was now temporarily homeless until he made it up to Canada.

As he handed in his room key, Timothy asked the motel owner for directions to the bus station.

"Where are you headed?" the lady inquired.

"I'm going north to visit a friend in Canada."

The woman offered to phone the bus depot regarding schedules and prices. The fares turned out to be quite enormous and Timothy couldn't mask his shock.

The motel owner then checked a travel site on her computer and advised Timothy that one-way fares from Shreveport to Syracuse, New York were even more outrageous, the lowest price being more than $700.

"Thanks for your assistance, ma'am, but I think I'll try my hand at hitchhiking. Those fares are well beyond my ability to pay."

"You're a priest, aren't you?"

"Yes, I've just retired."

"One of our guests mentioned that he's heading up to Shreveport today and he hasn't checked out yet. If you'd like, I can ask him if he minds driving you."

"Thank you so much. That would certainly get me started well on my way."

The owner called the guest's room, explained Timothy's dilemma, and arranged for the ride.

Fifteen minutes later the elderly gentleman entered the motel office to check out and introduced himself as Ralph Risely. He was an extremely pleasant man and insisted on treating Timothy to breakfast at a nearby diner. They finished eating just before ten o'clock and began the two hour drive to Shreveport.

When Ralph learned that Timothy was planning to hitchhike all the way to Canada, he found several maps in his glove box and gave them to Timothy, explaining that, "When you're relying on your thumb to travel, you need to know where you are and how to get to the next destination. Have you ever hitchhiked before?"

"Not since I was in university. It should be quite an adventure conversing with whichever folks happen to pick me up."

"It's pretty unusual these days to see anyone trying to bum a ride," Ralph commented. "Perhaps you need a gimmick. Why don't you rip off one of the flaps on that white box in the back seat and write on it in big letters 'PRIEST NEEDS RIDE' or something like that."

"That sounds like a great idea, Ralph, and it might encourage people to stop who like to talk about religion."

"It's illegal to hitchhike on the Interstates. You'll probably have to travel on the small highways, which means it's going to take you a lot longer to get anywhere."

"That's good to know although I'm really in no particular hurry. You're a fountain of useful knowledge, Ralph."

They made small talk for the next hour at which point Ralph sheepishly admitted, "I'm sort of a lapsed Catholic and generally make it to mass just at Christmas and Easter. It disturbs me that the church allows you to put yourself in danger when you travel. I thought they looked after their retired priests pretty well."

Timothy considered keeping his personal situation to himself but decided that he needed to hear the opinions of other Catholics about what had happened.

"I got in trouble with my Archbishop and he stripped me of all my priestly duties for disobeying his direct order. If I disclose the entire story, will you give me your honest reaction and not mince your words?"

Ralph agreed so Tim related the whole story about meeting the Canadian lawyer and developing doubts after their intense discussions about the Catholic Church. The priest then read out to Ralph the article that was printed in the community newspaper. Finally he explained the dire consequences that had ensued during his heated conversation with the Archbishop.

When he had concluded the saga, Timothy said, "Tell me the unvarnished truth, Ralph. Did I deserve to get banished from my church?"

Ralph didn't directly answer the question. Instead he said, "I guess I never realized that the life of a priest could be lonely. The priests at my church in Shreveport always seem to be surrounded by people."

"Larger churches require more than one priest," Timothy replied, "but my parish was tiny so I lived alone in the rectory."

"Didn't you pay into a pension plan?"

"No, the retired priests in my diocese are looked after through an unregistered fund and I had no legal right to any pension payments from it. I wouldn't have qualified for the pension anyway until I was seventy unless I had become too ill to carry out my duties. Fortunately I do qualify for government social security, which I'll start collecting in a few months when I turn sixty-five."

"No offense, Father, but why couldn't you save any money on your own?"

"I gave it all away during my career. Just like that family I saved from eviction a day before my trip to Las Vegas, there was always some parishioner desperate for temporary assistance which my diocese refused to provide. My lawyer friend from Canada called me an easy mark, but I felt I had no need to accumulate savings since my church would always be there to look after me in my old age."

"Will you read that article to me again?" Ralph asked.

Timothy did so.

"I'm not sure what to think of the 'milking widows' comment by the lawyer. That seems a bit harsh on the church, but I think you're bang on about being overworked and underpaid. Stripping you of your pension and salary over one episode of rebellion does appear to validate the attorney's opinion that the Catholic Church operates exactly like a heartless corporation. Look at the money it's going to save by summarily sacking you. That's just plain wrong. In fact I'd have to say honestly that what the church did to you makes me ashamed to call myself a Catholic."

They were now entering the southwestern limit of Shreveport. Ralph insisted on driving through the city so that he could drop Timothy off at the northeast end of Highway 79 in order to make it easier for Timothy to catch his next ride.

Tim thanked Ralph for the ride and for listening to his priestly predicament.

The priest sign worked like a charm and within a few minutes Timothy had secured a ride with two older ladies who chauffeured him to Minden. That trip was too short for much conversation.

This time Timothy had to walk a fair distance with his luggage before he reached the eastern outskirts of the town. His suitcase, which was relatively small, had wheels and a handle so Timothy could pull it along behind him with one hand while carrying the sports bag with the other.

Timothy wondered what people must think of him, walking along like a transient.

It was now almost three o'clock and Timothy looked at his maps of Louisiana and Arkansas. He decided to aim for El Dorado and stay there for his first night on this road trip.

He baked in the heat for over an hour before a young couple finally stopped.

Luck was with him because they were going to El Dorado for a rock concert and party. This pair wasn't at all inquisitive about why a priest was thumbing a ride. Timothy listened while they talked about concerts they had attended in the past.

They dropped Timothy off in front of the Flamingo Motel where he rented a room for the reasonable price of $46 plus tax.

Tim showered and then walked around the small city, and treated himself to supper at a fast food restaurant called Andy's.

He also purchased two postcards of El Dorado.

Arkansas was the fifth state Timothy had now seen in his lifetime.

Deeming it wise to take a page out of Boyd Billingsworth's playbook, Timothy counted his

money and jotted down each expense he had
incurred today.

He also began a trip journal in which he
noted who had given him rides and what sights
he had seen along the route.

Timothy went to bed quite elated. His
journey had progressed well on its opening day
and he had felt the thrill of being on an open
road adventure.

The next morning he awoke in a jubilant
mood, thirsting with anticipation as to what
today would bring. Timothy decided to wear his
priest's collar today in the hopes of
attracting rides more quickly. Drivers would
now be able to see both his sign and the
appropriate uniform.

The day was a bit overcast which was a
welcome relief from yesterday's blazing sun
and oppressive heat.

It took three separate rides with lengthy
waits in between before Timothy reached Pine
Bluff, and then he had to walk a long way
before he found a good spot to wait at the
east end of town for his next ride.

No wonder so few people hitchhiked these
days. It was an extremely inefficient mode of
travel.

The next phase of his journey was even
slower and after a long series of short hauls,
Timothy found himself in West Memphis,
Arkansas. It was almost eight o'clock by now
and Timothy decided to continue on to
Tennessee on the other side of the Mississippi
River so that he could spend the night in a
new state.

A ride finally came along just at dusk and
Timothy found himself deposited in the huge
city of Memphis after darkness had fallen.

He could see large buildings in the distance so he began walking in that direction.

Timothy hadn't proceeded half a dozen blocks when a disquieting feeling began to gnaw at him. Walking alone at night with luggage and a large amount of cash was foolhardy.

Like a magnet, Timothy began attracting unwanted attention and soon two figures were following him along a street in a run-down residential area of the city.

Before he had walked another block, the two men had overtaken him, eyeing Timothy carefully as they passed by. They soon disappeared just up ahead.

As Timothy arrived at the spot where the men had been, suddenly they appeared from behind some bushes.

"Give us your wallet and your watch and we won't hurt you," they demanded.

"I'm a poor Catholic priest. Surely you wouldn't stoop to robbing a man of the cloth."

"We don't discriminate," one of the thugs snarled. "Take out your wallet."

Timothy hadn't a clue what to do.

What a stupid old fool he was! He could be riding in the comfort and safety of a bus right now instead of being robbed and possibly murdered on this foreboding and darkened street.

"My wallet is in the larger suitcase," Timothy fibbed. "Please don't rob me."

Both men grabbed that suitcase and began impatiently tearing it open.

While their attention was momentarily diverted, Timothy began running for his life. He had a head start of almost fifty feet before the robbers noticed that he was fleeing. One of them took up pursuit leaving his mate to search for the wallet and anything else of value in the suitcase.

Timothy couldn't run at full speed with the sports bag so he was forced to drop it in on the sidewalk while he ran for his life, praying that someone would come along to help him.

As he rounded a corner with the much younger robber quickly gaining ground, a police car making its rounds suddenly appeared.

"Help, police, I'm being robbed," Timothy yelled. That got their attention and the cruiser stopped and began backing up quickly in order to get closer.

Both officers jumped out of the police car to ascertain what the problem was.

Timothy's pursuer caught sight of the cops and began fleeing in the opposite direction.

"That man and his accomplice are trying to rob me, officers. They've got my suitcase and now they want my wallet."

One of the officers jumped back in the car, pulled a U-turn and quickly sped off in pursuit of the thief. The other officer stayed with Timothy.

"I had to drop my sports bag a couple of blocks back so I could run faster," Timothy gasped. "The other thief is rummaging through my suitcase three or four blocks back. Everything I own is in those bags. Can we double back and try to find them?"

"Of course, sir; you can tell me what happened while we walk."

They began walking swiftly, retracing Timothy's route.

"I'm a Catholic priest. I've been hitchhiking for the past couple of days on my way up north to visit a friend. It was already after dark when I got dropped off in Memphis. I saw the outline of the tall buildings in the distance and decided to head in that direction. Two men accosted me and demanded my wallet. I ran away and by the grace of God, you arrived before they caught me. Look, there's my sports bag still on the sidewalk where I dropped it."

The sports bag was untouched. As they reached the next intersection, they saw the police car parked near the original scene of the crime.

When they reached the cruiser, the other officer was just returning.

"The perps ran off through the yards," the older cop explained. "I've called it in but they're probably long gone by now."

Timothy's suitcase was lying on the grass with his belongings strewn about.

"Let's round up your possessions," the younger officer suggested, "and we'll take your statement back at the station."

Timothy quickly stuffed his clothes back in his suitcase and rode back to the precinct in the back of the squad car. He had never before been in a police car and didn't much like the idea now.

As they made their way to the station, Timothy retold his story.

Both cops chastised Timothy for being out alone at night.

"You were damn lucky, Father. Where were you planning on staying tonight?"

"I was hoping to find an inexpensive motel."

"A gentleman your age shouldn't hitchhike," the older officer admonished. "How much money would the thieves have netted if they'd caught you?"

"I'm carrying about $1,400 in cash which represents my life savings. That's why I ran away rather than hand over my wallet. Maybe I'll have you take me to the bus station later instead of to a motel. I checked out the cost of bus fares and air fares to Canada when I was in DeRidder, Louisiana, but the prices were outrageous. Now that I've had this scare, I guess I'll have to bite the bullet and pay whatever it takes."

Nothing appeared missing other than a few small keepsakes which Timothy had received as gifts from parishioners. The officers took his statement and were kind enough to drive him to the main bus depot which was open all night.

Then the good news finally began trickling in. Fares were much cheaper from one major city to another, and Timothy purchased a one-way ticket from Memphis to Toronto for just over $200. It departed at midnight and Timothy would arrive in Toronto, Canada around six o'clock in the morning on Monday after a grueling ride of twenty-nine hours.

But at least Timothy would be safe!

As the bus pulled away exactly on time, Timothy gazed out at the lights of Memphis.

What devastation to his life would have been caused if the two thieves had successfully robbed him of his wallet and luggage! His passport had been packed in the suitcase and he might not have been able to cross into Canada without it.

Imagine being stranded in Memphis with no money, ID or belongings.

Timothy thanked God for protecting him from evil.

The long bus ride was mostly tedious although Timothy was excited when he caught a glimpse of Niagara Falls. He boarded a train from Toronto to Belleville and arrived there just after one-thirty in the afternoon on Monday.

Timothy looked at the large wall map of the city of Belleville and saw that Church Street was quite near. He exited the modern train station and began walking along Station Street.

He passed a large beer store and then walked along a river.

Soon he spotted the sign for Church Street and began walking up a hill and past an old stone Catholic cathedral with an adjoining beautiful and large modern rectory building.

About three short blocks further along, Timothy found 210 Church Street and was impressed.

The brickwork on the stately old building had obviously been freshly painted a deep rich red, and the trim was a lovely shade of pink.

Timothy's travel adventure was over.

This stately old building would be his home for the next little while.

Timothy opened the front door and found himself in a foyer.

He saw the sign for the law office of Boyd Billingsworth on the left hand inner door, so he opened it and stepped inside with his luggage, which he left in a waiting room at the end of a small hallway.

Tim poked his head into an office just inside an archway and an elderly secretary looked up and asked if she could assist him.

"Yes, thank you; I'm Timothy Camacho, here to see Mr. Billingsworth."

## CHAPTER 24 (A Tribute to Fluffy)

I called the local humane society in order to find out how best to dispose of Fluffy's body. They advised that I could bring him there and the lady also said that they'd be pleased to receive any cat cages, kitty litter or cat food that I no longer needed.

I rounded up all the cat paraphernalia from my apartment and from Jean's house and drove with Fluffy, wrapped in a towel, to the humane society facility.

The staff was most pleased to get all the pet items and a young girl showed me around the compound.

It was quite heartbreaking. The building was old and overcrowded with animals which were stuck in small cages waiting for adoption if they were lucky, or euthanasia if they were not.

The girl explained that since it was late spring, the cat population had exploded as so many litters of unwanted kittens had been brought in or, more commonly, dumped after hours outside the main entrance.

I asked to speak with the manager.

"It's been quite an eye-opener seeing the plight of these poor creatures," I admitted. "If you had surplus funds right now, how would you spend the money to improve the conditions for these animals?"

"This is such an old facility," the lady replied, "that there are many deficiencies. Our most pressing need is for a new septic system. We're not on municipal services out here in the country and our existing system is grossly inefficient and could break down completely at any time."

"How much would that cost?"

"We had a quote for $28,000 but we've been unable to get the funding."

"Is there anything else that the place is in dire need of?" I continued.

"The old building doesn't have air conditioning, so the place is very uncomfortable for both the staff and the animals in the summertime."

"How much do you estimate that might cost?"

"Again, we had a rough quote of $12,000 a couple of years back for a combined furnace and air conditioning system, but our budget can't accommodate such an expense at this time."

"I noticed that the animals, especially the cats, are crammed two or three together into tiny cages with their food right beside the litter trays. There's barely enough room for the poor things to lie down. Surely there must be a better way to house them."

"If we had the money, sir, and a larger facility, then we could install much larger two-level cat cages with the litter tray on the lower level and the food and cat baskets on the upper tier. Some of the pricier caging systems can even incorporate access to an individual enclosed exterior area to enable the animals to actually sit outdoors in the fresh air. Those sophisticated cages could only be installed, however if a new addition was constructed."

"Is there space on this property to construct such an expansion?" I inquired.

"Oh yes; we have oodles of unused land behind the building."

While the lady and I were talking, the pitiful sounds of crying animals filled the air. I found this setup intolerable and was relieved that I had brought Fluffy to my apartment rather than abandoning him in this forlorn place. The thought had actually crossed my mind to discard him here. The only thing that stopped me was my fear that Jean would recover quickly and remove me as her legal representative when she discovered how treacherous I really was.

"How large an addition would be required to permit those superior cages for the number of cats and small dogs you have here now?"

"My best guess is that we'd need an addition of approximately 1,500 square feet which would entail construction costs of roughly $120,000. It would cost several thousand dollars more for the fancy cages. The dog enclosures for the larger breeds could also be drastically improved at the same time for a few thousand more."

"I'm beginning to understand," I said as an idea began taking shape in my mind. "Can you think of anything else that would improve the everyday lives of these animals?"

"The existing staff doesn't have the time to play with the animals or even take the dogs out for walks. Some kindly local people volunteer their time so a lucky few dogs and cats do receive a bit of individual human affection. If the funding were available, I'd love to hire students part-time to interact with the animals."

"That does seem like a wonderful idea," I interjected. "Not only would the students earn a bit of money but they'd also learn to care for animals. What about your pet adoption system? Could it be improved to get more cats and dogs back out into a proper home?"

"It's gotten so costly to spay and neuter the animals that many people are put off

180

taking on a pet," the woman responded. "A special fund to offset those costs would encourage folks of limited means, especially seniors, to adopt a pet."

"You've certainly got a difficult situation here right now," I said. "I'd like to do something to alleviate the most urgent deficiencies you're currently faced with. If I was prepared to donate $300,000 to this facility, would you and your board be willing to commit to incorporating all of the renovations and improvements for the animals that we've just talked about?"

The woman's jaw dropped.

I was dressed in an expensive grey suit and even though she had no idea that I was a successful attorney, I exuded the aura of financial prosperity.

The manager knew I wasn't kidding.

"Definitely, sir!"

"I have one minor request, ma'am. In consideration of the donation, I'd like a small plaque put up somewhere near the doorway of the new addition naming it the 'Jean Powers and Fluffy Cat Room'. Jean is a recently deceased client of mine and Fluffy was her beloved pet."

"We'd be most honored to remember Jean and Fluffy with such an appropriate tribute, sir."

"Excellent! Here's my business card. Please contact me as soon as your board gives its approval in principle to my proposals, and I'll come around with the certified check."

"That's just wonderful, Mr. Billingsworth. I'll try to convene a special meeting immediately, and I'll call you just as soon as we've given these tremendous improvements the preliminary okay."

I drove back to the office immensely pleased with this turn of events. It was by far the most money I'd ever spent at one time and I was puzzled wondering what had happened to my imbedded frugality.

A few hours later I was in my office with Martina when Florence opened my door and announced that a Mr. Camacho was here to see me.

I introduced Timothy to the two ladies and then brought him up to the apartment to show him his quarters.

He insisted that I go back downstairs to work.

CHAPTER 25 (Friends Reunited)

For supper Timothy and I had a pizza delivered.

After we had demolished it, I suggested that we drink beer and catch each other up on the momentous events in our lives since we had parted company in Las Vegas.

I went first and tried to explain the vague reasons for my life-altering decision to retire.

I also told Timothy about my encounter with Bea in the parkette in Las Vegas and how she also became my temporary roommate at the El Cortez.

"I strode past her determined to mind my own business, but by the time I reached the hotel entrance, I stopped to ask myself what Timothy would do. Knowing full well that you would do whatever it took to help her, I went back across the street to talk to her. By doing that I rescued Beatrice from what would have been at best a very uncomfortable night and at worst even real danger stranded alone and vulnerable in the cold night. Not only that, but I showed her a good time in Las Vegas by squiring her around. She gushed that it was the most wonderful few days of her life. It amazes me how spending one week with a priest has significantly changed me for the better."

I didn't divulge my pending gift to the local animal shelter, preferring to keep that inexplicable burst of generosity strictly between me and Fluffy.

After a solid hour, it was finally Timothy's turn to speak and he related in detail the incident leading up to his firing followed by his adventuresome stab at hitchhiking.

When he had finished, I remarked, "Your influence on me has been entirely positive, but my effect on you seems to have been disastrous."

"Strangely enough, I don't view it that way. Since I was evicted from the rectory, all the stress and strain of decades of overwork have been lifted off my shoulders. Despite the Archbishop's disgust with my recent conduct, I've concluded that I can be rightfully proud of my career as a Catholic priest. I never succumbed to the perverted temptations which sometimes plagued some of my fellow priests, and I always tried to be true to what I perceived as God's will. My obvious failing has been my propensity to drink too much and feel sorry for myself because of the loneliness."

"I do appreciate what you've just said, Timothy, but you got fired for raising matters with your church that I complained to you were unjust. My arrogant criticism of you for blindly accepting the church's shoddy treatment as your employer seems to have ruined your life."

"That's not the way to look at these events, Boyd. You made me step back and reexamine my life as a priest. By doing that I was able to satisfy myself that I did not knowingly try to persuade vulnerable parishioners to give their money to the church. In that regard, I wish that I had spoken with you when I was a young priest. Until we had our discussion about priestly influence, I was completely unaware that I was even in a position to pressure people into doing things they might not really want to do.

Now I realize that a priest should weigh carefully the opposing interests of the church and the individual parishioner. You simply removed my blinders."

"But it seems, Timothy, that I also turned you into some sort of radical. That's the aspect of our brief association which has now harmed you."

"I don't regret my recent bout of speaking out publicly about my church. I've come to believe that in fact I wasn't treated fairly. It's not a sin to make one's legitimate concerns known. Turning the other cheek doesn't mean permitting oneself to be a doormat. My church is at fault for refusing to discuss these issues with me, and the Archbishop's abrupt termination of my employment was an obscene and unjust overreaction. In no way are you at fault?"

"I'd be willing to finance a lawsuit against the Catholic Church to recapture your pension money and to get you reinstated as a priest if you believe that would right the wrongs. Suing them would also raise public awareness to the issues of overwork and insufficient pay."

"That's most kind of you, Boyd, and I must admit that I have briefly considered such an action, but it doesn't feel like the right thing to do. I have faith that God is with me throughout all of this personal turmoil. I'm not going to be forever mute about my treatment either. When I get back to Texas I fully intend to speak out again. As a former priest, I won't be under the pressure that working priests face to keep their mouths shut or face the consequences."

Just then the telephone rang.

It was Corbett calling to chat. I told him that my houseguest had arrived and we arranged for the three of us to meet at Jim's condo the following evening for beer and fellowship.

Timothy was quite exhausted from his long bus journey so we hit the sack early.

On Tuesday after supper Timothy and I walked over to Corbett's where I made the introductions.

For a while the three of us just made small talk.

As the number of beer we drank rose, the subject of our careers came up. Jim asked Timothy how he felt now that his role as a priest was behind him.

"I feel nothing but pride, Jim. I'm satisfied that I carried out my functions over those thirty-nine years diligently and honestly. The fact that I got the boot at the end of my career and that as a result I have no money or assets to show for a lifetime job isn't important. Obviously I never became a priest for the material benefits. I truly believe that at all times I was a credit to the priesthood and a devout servant of God."

Corbett seemed quite impressed with that point of view and retorted, "I feel precisely the same way. I was always a kind and honest lawyer but not very successful monetarily. I'd drop my fee for any clients going through a rough patch financially, or I'd accept their promises to pay me later, which they rarely did. I refused to get involved with crooked realtors or mortgage brokers. The course of professional behavior I chose to follow wasn't the road to riches, but in retrospect I'm nothing but pleased that I avoided the many temptations to stray off that path of integrity."

Jim turned to me.

"Slimy, how do you feel now that your legal career is almost over?"

I thought seriously about the question for a moment before replying.

"I've accumulated all the wealth I could ever need and then some, but the sense of pride the two of you now cherish has eluded me. I've got to live with the fact that I've been a user and a manipulator since shortly after Gabriela died. I'm at least pleased that I've milked my last widow. The old girls are safe from me now."

Timothy interjected.

"Boyd, it's how you conduct yourself from this moment onward that will determine how you finally view yourself. That's especially true if you ask forgiveness for your past transgressions."

"Sorry, Timothy, but I'm a non-believer so I certainly won't be seeking God's absolution for my conduct. At least I'm wrapping up my legal practice in a good way. I could have sold my business to one of the big firms and made some money, but that would mean that I was just transferring my clients from one shark to another. Instead I'm giving my files to honest young lawyers who will look after the clients properly. That's definitely a result of your influence and at least that's one decision that has provided me with a bit of self-satisfaction."

It was well after midnight by the time Timothy and I said goodnight to Corbett.

It had been a most enjoyable and beer-saturated evening, but it had also made me uneasy with the notion that Jim and Timothy were in fact much richer than I was. Their

genuine pride in their past careers was worth
much more than my bulging truckloads of money.

## CHAPTER 26 (Return of the Strange Dream)


A few days after our visit with Corbett, I received a call from the animal shelter. The board of directors had approved spending my donation as discussed.

I delivered a certified check to the shelter and asked that my name as donor be kept anonymous. They agreed to show the donor as Fluffy Powers.

I did however have the charitable receipt issued in my name.

As the weeks passed, one by one my estates were finalized. Martina had obtained the Certificate of Appointment for Jean Powers' estate on May 30$^{th}$, which meant that the conditional Offer on her house could be firmed up. I was also able to move the closing date up to Friday, June 13$^{th}$.

The sale of Jean's personal possessions took place within days of receiving the certificate.

Timothy loved his new freedom and we spent many an evening over at Corbett's condo discussing the world's problems.

My sleep had been free of nightmares ever since the night before Fluffy died.

On Friday, June 6$^{th}$ I was walking downtown to my bank, pleased that my self-image was rapidly improving.

That all changed in an instant.

While waiting at the corner of Pinnacle and Bridge for the traffic light to change, I happened to be standing behind two men and couldn't help but overhear their conversation.

"My elderly aunt died yesterday," the taller man mentioned. "She named me as the

Estate Trustee so I'll have to find a good lawyer to handle the legal work on the estate. Do you have any recommendations?"

His friend's answer pierced my heart like a bullet.

"Whatever you do, don't use that shyster Billingsworth up on Church Street. He did my mother's estate a few years ago and charged more than $75,000. Mom trusted that guy implicitly and he turned around and robbed her after she was dead."

That night the horrible dream returned.

This time I was up on the witness stand. Jim Corbett began to question me.

"Did you recognize any of the prosecution's witnesses, Mr. Billingsworth?"

"Yes, I remembered most of them."

"Were they embellishing their testimony?"

"I guess not. They all seemed to have a pretty good handle on their files. I didn't recall a lot of the specific details they were complaining about, but I don't dispute their version of my conduct."

Corbett then announced, "I have no further questions."

I looked quizzically at Jim, who was standing just a few feet from me.

"Whose side are you on, Jim?" I whispered angrily.

"You did just fine," he replied.

"Are you out of your mind? All I did was corroborate the prosecution's evidence. What kind of defense is that?"

"But you told the truth, Slimy. Most lawyers would have tried to lie their way out of the accusations by flatly denying them or blaming their staff."

The Devil's advocate stood up and hissed, "We wish to pose some questions in cross-examination."

"Very well, proceed," boomed the voice from behind the waterfall veil.

At first I was petrified with worry about what questions this horned prosecutor would ask me, but that fear quickly gave way to anger. I sensed that this horrid shyster was going to bully me into some sort of confession. I thought of Father Timothy and his out-of-character rebellion when his church tried to intimidate him into retracting his complaints.

"Mr. Billingsworth, are you not ashamed of having cheated all of these vulnerable, trusting elderly ladies?"

"I didn't cheat any of them. Every single one of them knew in advance how much I would be charging their estate for my professional services."

"Did they also know that you would renege on so many of your specific promises to them?"

"Of course not; as Estate Trustee it was my duty to make tough decisions for the good of the beneficiaries. Sometimes that meant failing to honor some of the verbal requests that my clients had made. Assuring them that everything would work out smoothly and precisely as they wished was just part of my job. Those old ladies would have worried themselves sick if I had left doubts in their minds about their affairs. Did you not notice that not a single one of those dissatisfied clients you paraded up here alleged that I failed to carry out the specific terms of their written Wills?"

"I certainly noticed how upset they all were that you had blatantly lied to them. Can you provide this Court with the name of even one client whose verbal wishes you did fulfill honorably even though it wasn't spelled out in the Will?"

"No," I answered firmly.

"In that case, I have no further questions, Your Honor," the horned prosecutor proclaimed.

The Judge then spoke from behind the waterfall.

"If as you stated, Mr. Corbett, that this is your sole witness, then I am ready to render my judgment."

Corbett had a glum expression on his face as he answered morosely, "Very well, Your Honor."

From my perch on the witness stand, I saw the Jesus panhandler fold up his notebook and quietly leave the courtroom.

At the same time, the prosecutor and his sidekicks began giving each other high fives.

That meant to me that I was doomed and I heaved a huge sigh of resignation. It was obvious that I was about to be sentenced to an eternity in Hell.

Suddenly Fluffy jumped up on the barristers' table and stood erect on his hind legs. It made for a ridiculous spectacle since he was still decked out in his miniature legal robes.

Little Grey did the same thing and shocked me even further by announcing in a tiny squeaky voice, "If it pleases this Court, we have some rebuttal questions for the accused."

I was dumbstruck by the hilarity of the whole scene. My little furry friends were still trying to save me from damnation.

The prosecution team immediately ceased their celebrations and the lead lawyer quickly objected to any further questions being allowed.

At that moment I woke up covered in sweat.

CHAPTER 27 (Road Trip)

Although Timothy was still greatly enjoying his new freedom, I observed him beginning to get antsy about what to do with the rest of his life.

On June 14$^{th}$ while we were having our regular Saturday night beer fest at Corbett's condo, Timothy announced, "Boyd, I've thoroughly enjoyed and appreciated being able to stay with you here in Belleville, but last night I had a dream. I believe that God wants me to return to Bleakwood although I don't yet understand what plans He has for me."

"My legal practice is virtually closed now," I replied, "which brings up an interesting thought. I'm in the mood for a driving trip, something to reward myself for having the good sense to retire while I'm still young enough to enjoy life. How would you like to accompany me on a meandering route back to Texas?"

"Are you just saying that to provide me with a cheap means of getting back home?" Timothy asked.

"No; I've been pondering what to do as a retirement reward, and I want to see Newfoundland which is an island off Canada's extreme east coast. From there we could make our way south and eventually veer west and on to Texas. It might take us a month to complete the whole trip."

Corbett chimed in, "That sounds like a tremendous adventure. If my health wasn't so precarious, I would have loved to join you."

By then we were each on our fifth beer and I couldn't pass up this perfect chance to be sarcastic.

"Thank God you're an invalid, Patsy. Spending a month with you would be a bloody penalty, not a reward."

He quickly retorted, "That's a good point, Slimy. A month of your bullshit would probably kill me. I truly feel sorry for this poor priest friend of ours. He's about to taste a month in Hell."

All three of us broke into fits of intoxicated laughter over that saucy exchange.

Over the next couple of weeks, Timothy and I with Corbett's help plotted out a tentative trip route.

Early in July I attended at the office of an older colleague and redid my own Will. I hadn't even bothered to change it when Gabriela died in 1987. Lawyers are often the worst people to look after their own legal affairs.

I left my office building and $150,000 to the three women attorneys and named them as my Estate Trustees. I bequeathed $150,000 to Corbett, another $150,000 to Timothy and gave old Florence $100,000 so that she wouldn't have to work any longer. It was difficult to decide what to do with the bulk of my estate. In the end I divided that residue in varying percentage shares among the local humane society, library and hospital as well as smaller local charities.

Since Belleville had been my lifelong home, it was important to me to give back to my community. In life I may have sucked out as much cash from the citizens of the city as I could by charging such whopping legal fees, but in death I felt a need to give back something.

It was now my intention to give away a goodly portion of my wealth while I was still living. My recent gift to the humane society had filled me with a deep sense of pride, knowing that I had truly made a difference to those unfortunate and unwanted animals.

I had Martina put my new Will in her firm's safety deposit box and advised her that I had named the three lawyers as my trustees.

My next task was completed at my bank where I set up a tax-free annuity in US funds in the amount of $36,000 per year, payable monthly, for Timothy Camacho. I had obtained his social security number and bank account details on the pretext of requiring the information in the event I had to wire some money down to us once we reached Texas.

I pushed the ladies to wrap up all the remaining tag ends from my estate files and by July 4th everything had been completed, even Jean Powers' income tax returns. I had never administered an estate so quickly.

I signed a limited Power of Attorney allowing the three lawyers together to sign any remaining estate documentation on my behalf.

As a result of all that hard work, my presence in Belleville was no longer required.

Timothy and I had our usual Saturday night party at Corbett's condo and then the priest and I began our road trip in my uncomfortable Little Chevy on a blistering hot Sunday with no air conditioning.

Since my car was getting quite long in the tooth, I opted to stay on smaller highways in order to keep our speed down and not overly tax the car's engine. A 2002 compact car was not built for the high speeds required to keep up with traffic on the freeways.

Despite his fervent objections, I insisted that Timothy accept $2,000 in cash, half in

Canadian funds and the remainder in US money, so that he could enjoy this trip without having to deplete his own paltry savings.

By late afternoon on our first day we took a motel room in the tiny Quebec village of Yamachiche.

We drove around the small community and Timothy noticed a lovely and historic Catholic cathedral. We parked the car and walked around the cemetery adjacent to the church.

A priest saw us and strolled over. Fortunately he spoke English, and when he discovered that Timothy was a retired priest, he insisted on giving us a tour of the church.

On a bulletin board inside there were various notices and I asked the priest, Father Leo Desaulniers, to translate a couple of them.

One was a plea for donations to enable children to attend a two-week camping excursion beginning in a few days. The priest lamented that there were twelve children who had signed up but wouldn't be able to go after all because their parents couldn't afford the $200 fee and insufficient funds had been raised by the church in its campaign.

While Timothy was off by himself admiring the decorative font, I wrote a check to the church and handed it to Father Leo, explaining that this was our small way of thanking him for his kindness in providing us with a tour of his lovely church.

As a beaming Father Leo waved goodbye, Timothy remarked at how pleased the priest seemed that we had dropped by.

"Perhaps he was lonely and grateful that he had someone to talk with for a few minutes," I replied, not wanting to tell Timothy about my little gift to the kids.

Two nights later Timothy and I were waiting in line at the ferry terminal in North Sydney, Nova Scotia to make the overnight trip to Newfoundland.

For the next twelve days we did an extensive tour of the island, including driving all the way north to St. Anthony to see the location of the ancient Viking settlement.

We left Little Chevy in St. Barbe while we took a passenger ferry back to the mainland and spent a night in a bed and breakfast inn at Forteau, Labrador. Few Canadians and almost no Americans ever get to see that remote area of Canada.

On the way back south to the main highway, we toured Gros Morne National Park.

The highlight of the Newfoundland portion of our trip was a two-night excursion to the French islands of St. Pierre and Miquelon. We stayed both nights in the historic Hotel Robert and learned that Al Capone had stayed at that hotel during the prohibition era.

Capone was apparently a lieutenant in the mob at that time and had been sent to the island to discover why so many shipments of illicit liquor were being confiscated by the feds.

He concluded that the rattling of the bottles in the wooden packing crates was alerting the authorities to the rum-running boats.

From then on the bottles were packed in cloth bags filled with straw.

As a point of historical trivia, our tour guide informed us that the locals used those discarded wooden crates to build homes, one of which was still standing and occupied today.

My 67$^{th}$ birthday fell on Saturday, July 26$^{th}$ and we celebrated that minor event in Fredericton, New Brunswick where we took a tour of the provincial parliament building.

Very early the next morning we crossed into the USA at Vanceboro, Maine.

Just before eleven o'clock we happened to come upon a Catholic church in the small village of Old Town.

Parishioners were parking in an empty lot across the small highway from the church and it was obvious that a mass was soon to commence.

Timothy requested that we stop because he wanted to attend the mass and take communion. Since it was just starting to rain, I decided to join him inside rather than sit in the car.

After the service, Timothy wanted to speak with the priest so I tagged along. To my mild surprise, Timothy asked the priest to join us for lunch.

We found a restaurant just up the road and over the next hour Timothy related to Father Andre the events which had converged and then exploded causing Timothy's termination as a priest in Texas.

Timothy showed Father Andre the article from the community newspaper and pointed out that I was the shady lawyer who had raised the issue of abusive employment practices by the Catholic Church.

Father Andre appeared to give the matter a lot of reflection before he finally responded.

"I certainly agree that my fellow priests and I are tremendously overworked. Our Catholic Church is attempting to alleviate the situation in various ways such as importing priests from third world countries, but effective reforms always seem to take far too long. When they do finally come, it's been my opinion that often they're watered-down versions of what is truly required. Personally it's difficult for me to equate the obscene hours I work with the concept that the church is purposely taking advantage of me. Have you in fact reached that conclusion yourself, Father Timothy?"

"Not entirely," Tim responded. "I was driven merely to ask the question but the Archbishop refused even to discuss it with me. Mr. Billingsworth here has suggested that I commence a lawsuit on the basis that the Catholic Church has violated its legal obligations as my employer by terminating me without compensation or notice. I can't in good conscience sue my own church, but I do believe that I've been treated unfairly and overly harshly just because I raised the issue in a public forum."

"I fully agree with your assessment in that regard," Father Andre commented. "We shouldn't be punished for raising legitimate doubts about any issue facing our church. Non-Catholics like Mr. Billingsworth here are regularly calling some of our traditional customs and practices into question. Our church shouldn't be stifling honest discussion by threatening to yank our pensions if we persist."

Father Andre then turned to me.

"Boyd, the other issue you raised about the church milking widows is certainly controversial. Did you really mean that?"

"My own conduct as a smooth lawyer who took advantage of my elderly clients was certainly deliberate. I attended various church services for the sole purpose of scrounging up more wealthy clients. I truly

was in the business of milking widows. My
suspicion for many years has been that priests
and ministers are essentially doing the same
thing and are diabolically efficient at it.
Father Timothy doesn't believe that the
Catholic Church has the greedy motives that I
accuse it of. Looking back at your own
practices, do you believe that you
inappropriately influenced vulnerable elderly
parishioners to remember the Catholic Church
in their Wills?"

"You lawyers have a knack of phrasing
things in a most aggravating way. Let's just
say that, like Father Timothy, I've never
examined my conduct in that light, so I'm not
able to answer your question honestly off the
top of my head. I will say though in my
defense, that any subtle pressure I
inadvertently exerted was done in the sincere
belief that it was the right thing to do in
order to further God's work in this world.
I'll certainly reexamine my actions in that
regard retroactively over the next little
while, and I pray that I don't conclude that
you may be correct. That's as truthful an
answer as I'm capable of providing at this
moment."

Timothy thanked his fellow priest for
being candid, and we continued on our journey.

That night we made it as far as Portland.

We kept to the shoreline highways wherever
possible and spent Monday night in Boston
where we had a chance to take a walk around
the historic section of that city.

For the sole purpose of being able to say
that we had been there, Timothy and I drove
through New York City on Wednesday morning but
were too uncomfortable even to stop for gas or
a meal. We crossed the bridge into New Jersey

and made our way to Atlantic City where we got a hotel room for three nights at the Taj Mahal.

On the first night I had another dream, but this one did not have a courtroom setting.

Fluffy and Little Grey both appeared as furry little angels with halos, and they wordlessly flew me to an animal shelter where a large poster on the front door explained that Hurricane Sandy a couple of years earlier had devastated many homes in the city which resulted in the shelters being overrun with lost and abandoned cats and dogs. Inside the shelter it was bedlam as the facility was absolutely inundated with animals, often resulting in three or four cats sharing a small cage. The noise of the crying and whining animals was soul destroying.

I was actually crying when I woke up.

On Thursday morning after breakfast, while Timothy went for a long walk along the boardwalk, I asked directions to the nearest animal shelter.

When I found it, I was stunned to see that the exact poster from my dream was nailed up on the front door. The interior was also precisely as I had been shown in my dream.

I had to do something. This was so much more than coincidence.

I spoke at length with the director of the shelter and discovered that the facility was in desperate need of renovations but lacked the funding.

The situation here was even more appalling than at the tiny shelter in Belleville.

I called my bank from the shelter and arranged for the transfer of a million dollars in US funds to the shelter's account.

My only request was that the facility made
some sort of acknowledgement that the bequest
was donated in memory of Jean Powers from
Canada and her beloved cat Fluffy together
with Little Grey, a cat from Ozona, Texas.

As before, I didn't mention to Timothy
what I had done. My generosity to the animals
was my own solemn secret.

After our stay in Atlantic City, we drove
slowly south to Virginia Beach and then veered
west.

We spent one night in Selma, Alabama where
we wandered through the church from which
Martin Luther King Jr. had begun his march for
freedom back in the 1960's.

Timothy was excited each time we entered a
new state, so we headed due south and spent a
night in Pensacola, Florida.

My gambling urges returned and I insisted
on spending a couple of nights in Biloxi,
Mississippi at one of the casino hotels.

I made a small donation of $5,000 to an
animal shelter there.

The final night of our trip, Thursday,
August 14th, found us staying in DeRidder,
Louisiana in the same motel where Timothy had
briefly resided after being dismissed by the
Catholic Church.

Our fantastic road trip together was over.

CHAPTER 28 (Priestly Security)

As we ate a nice supper in DeRidder, I
asked Timothy, "Now that you're back home,
where do you think you'd like to live?"

"Bleakwood has been my place of residence
for the past thirty-five years. I was assigned
to that church just four years after my
ordination and remained there continually
until the Archbishop terminated my employment.
I'm not sure how I'm going to afford to rent
anything, but now that I'm back in Texas I can
apply for my social security. I'm confident
that God will direct me and take care of me.
Bleakwood is the only place that feels like my
home."

"But you mentioned once that you had no
relatives or friends here," I replied. "Don't
you worry about being ostracized now that
everyone knows you were sacked by the church?
People might assume that there was some sordid
reason for your dismissal."

"It's true that I don't have any close
friends in Bleakwood, but everyone knows me
here because of my long association with the
church. I intend to tell the truth about why I
was let go and let the people decide for
themselves whether to shun me."

"I guess this is as good a time as any to
tell you what I've done," I answered. "Before
we left Canada I purchased an annuity for you.
It's already done and can't be cancelled, so
please accept my gift with pleasure. On the
first day of every month for as long as you
live, the insurance company will deposit
$3,000 into your bank account in Jasper. I've
structured it so that the payments to you are
not taxable, and your first payment will
arrive on September 1st. Now that you have a

stable income, hopefully your accommodation options will be much better."

Timothy was thunderstruck and simply sat there gaping at me.

"There's one more thing that I've done. It's my parting gift to you for changing my life for the better and making me into a much nicer version of myself. I want you to be able to live in your own home free of any worry about greedy landlords. Just before my birthday I arranged for $120,000 in US funds to be deposited into your bank account. That should enable you to purchase a modest home in the Bleakwood area and get yourself a small car and some furniture. Tomorrow we'll drive over to Jasper and make sure that the money transfer has been made. Then I'll chauffeur you around car and house shopping."

"I'm rendered speechless," Timothy stammered.

"Your God has indeed been looking after you, Timothy. The only anomaly is why He selected a life-long scoundrel like me to be the conduit."

Timothy excused himself to go to the washroom. When he returned a few minutes later, I knew that he had been crying.

He graciously thanked me for my generosity and expressed his everlasting gratitude.

Back in our room, we drank beer and reminisced about the wonderful driving trip we had just completed.

The following morning, being Friday, we drove into Jasper. The money had arrived flawlessly. We got a motel room for two nights and drove around to car dealerships and real estate offices.

There was one listing right in the tiny village of Bleakwood so we checked it out immediately with the realtor.

It was a very basic stucco bungalow with a detached garage and was listed at $85,000.

Timothy loved the location which was just two doors away from the Catholic church, and he submitted a cash offer that same afternoon.

The vendor accepted Tim's offer on the spot and included the furniture and contents with the sale. The house had belonged to the vendor's late mother and had been vacant for the past three months.

Since the seller knew Timothy personally, he even agreed that Tim could move in immediately without waiting for the closing date so long as he transferred the utilities into his name on Monday.

That evening Timothy found a small late-model used car to his liking and purchased it. The dealer promised to have it ready for pick-up the following afternoon.

That Friday night I had another dream, this one quite short.

Fluffy and Little Grey again appeared as tiny angels and wordlessly conveyed the message that it was now time for me to return home.

On Saturday morning over breakfast I informed Timothy about the dream and said that I would begin my drive home to Canada on Sunday morning.

We picked up Timothy's car on Saturday afternoon.

Timothy treated me to supper and beer at a pub near our motel to celebrate the end of our trip together.

After we had polished off the food with one pitcher of beer, Tim ordered another.

"Boyd, something you said when we were visiting Jim Corbett has been bothering me, but out of respect for your privacy and personal beliefs, I've never mentioned it. Tonight is the last opportunity we'll have to discuss it face to face."

"Sure, Timothy; what was it that I said?"

"You indicated that you didn't believe in God and wouldn't be seeking His forgiveness for any sins you may have committed as a lawyer. Since I'm both a priest and a devout Catholic, that statement horrified me. Although I've been stripped of my priestly duties by the Archbishop, I'm still an ordained priest and believe that I'm still fully able to administer the sacraments. When we get back to the motel, if you're willing, I'd be honored to hear your confession and absolve you of your sins even though you're not a Catholic."

I paused for several moments before responding, trying to collect my thoughts and assess Timothy's offer from every angle.

"That's very caring of you to offer, Father Timothy, and I want to try to explain my reasoning before I give you an answer. I'm not a full-fledged atheist. I'm some variation of an agnostic because I have no firm idea what if anything I believe in. If there is a God who made me, then He must realize that He didn't provide me with the intellect necessary to understand His plan for me. If a firm belief in God and Jesus is a requirement of being admitted into Heaven, then it's God's fault for making me incapable of detecting His presence. I have serious reservations believing that God would make Heaven such an exclusive resort. In fact, I do believe that many devout people actually perpetrate evil by being so inflexible in their intolerance of those who don't share the same faith. It seems that most wars and genocides have been caused by overly pious religions."

I paused so that Timothy could evaluate what I had just said.

"None of us truly understands God's mysteries, Boyd. I certainly don't even though I've studied His Holy Word during my entire adult life. In my humble opinion, what you've just disclosed doesn't preclude you from taking confession."

"I needed you to realize, Timothy, that for the reasons I articulated, I'd feel like a fraud confessing to a God I don't believe in. On the other hand, I consider you to be my true and valued friend. If hearing my confession is important for your peace of mind, then I'm willing to do it."

"Let's go for it," Timothy answered as he poured the last bit of beer into our glasses.

Then he joked, "It might be the first time in history that a drunken defrocked priest has taken confession from a drunken attorney who preyed on trusting old widows."

Back in the motel room, Timothy donned his priestly garments and I honestly confessed that I was truly sorry for the way I had conducted my law practice.

Timothy admitted just before we turned the lights out that he felt greatly relieved now that my sins had been forgiven.

I just felt good that I had made him happy by going through a ritual that was so important to his faith.

CHAPTER 29 (Homeward Bound)

On Sunday morning we slept in and had just enough time for a quick breakfast before Timothy needed to leave in order to take in the final mass of the day at a nearby Catholic church.

We said our goodbyes just before eleven o'clock and I fired up Little Chevy to begin the long drive back home.

Because of my late start, I only made it as far as Texarkana where I got a motel room for the night.

The next day, being Monday, I got as far as Memphis when Little Chevy's engine virtually exploded. Fortunately I was in town on a quiet commercial street so I was able to ease the little beast over to the curb.

I opened the hood and knew immediately that the whole motor was toast.

There was a hotel just down the street so I walked there with my luggage and booked a room for the night.

I arranged to have my car towed and rode in the tow truck to their storage yard. The owner was on the premises and confirmed the obvious. Little Chevy was beyond repair. I signed the old car over to him for the price of the tow and a ride back to my hotel, and said goodbye to my long-time vehicular buddy.

This hotel provided a regular free shuttle to the Memphis airport so I jumped on board to check out flights to Toronto. I managed to book a flight at a reasonable price for the following morning with a connection in Chicago.

As I was filling my time in the late afternoon walking around that area of the city, I happened by a small animal shelter and walked in.

As the manager showed me through the place, the plight of these poor animals deeply moved me. I called my bank and arranged for the immediate transfer of $300,000 to the facility.

Although giving the donation made me feel good, I still returned to my hotel with a broken heart.

As rich as I was, the plight of abandoned and stray animals was enormous.

I fully realized that my entire fortune would be a mere drop in the bucket of money required to eradicate the needless suffering of those innocent creatures throughout North America.

I took some solace in the fact that at least I had genuinely assisted a few of them.

In the evening I phoned Corbett and told him about the untimely demise of Little Chevy.

We had a great chat which cheered me immensely. Jim was a true and loyal friend.

That night the courtroom dream returned at precisely the same point at which the previous nightmare had concluded.

Fluffy and Little Grey were standing on the barristers' table wearing their miniature robes, and I was on the witness stand.

I noted that the panhandler from Las Vegas with the large wardrobe of orange shirts was not in attendance. I chuckled to myself wondering if his shirt now bore the message "JESUS HAS LEFT THE BUILDING".

In fact the courtroom was completely empty except for the lawyers and me.

The Judge's voice boomed out that he would allow the rebuttal questions despite the objection from the prosecutor.

Fluffy spoke in his tiny squeaky voice.

"You testified that you couldn't provide the name of even one solitary client for whom you carried out faithfully both the written terms of the Will and any accompanying verbal requests."

"That's correct," I answered.

"Your Honor, I submit that Mr. Billingsworth was not truthful in that response."

The prosecutor sprung up and objected.

"Judge, the accused's counsel cannot contradict the testimony of their own witness. That's my job and I don't want to pursue this line of questioning."

"The prosecution is correct on that point," the Judge commented.

"With respect, Your Honor," Fluffy squeaked, "it was the prosecution which asked that question and I intend to prove that the accused's answer was incorrect."

"In that case I'll allow it," the Judge ruled.

Fluffy continued.

"Was Jean Powers one of your clients?"

"Yes," I replied.

"Tell this Court how you failed to fulfill either the terms of her written Will or any of her verbal requests."

"In the end I did comply with her instructions, both oral and written, although at the time she signed her Will, I had no intention of abiding by her verbal wishes."

"What made you change your mind?"

"Jean wanted me to take care of her beloved cat just like I had falsely promised to do. I would have just dumped it at the local humane society except that I was fearful that Jean might recover from her stroke and remove me as her Estate Trustee and Power of Attorney when she discovered that I had abandoned her pet."

That didn't appear to be the answer that Fluffy had hoped for and he was clearly flustered.

Jim Corbett saw that his assistant was floundering, so he stood up and asked, "Was it not in fact the time you spent in Las Vegas with a Catholic priest that made you change the way you ran your law practice? Was it living with that kindly and compassionate priest that persuaded you to mend your ways and begin honoring all of your clients' requests?"

The lead prosecutor again jumped up to object before I could open my mouth.

"Objection; counsel is deliberately ignoring the clear testimony of his own client and is now trying to put contrary words into his mouth."

"Objection sustained," ruled the Judge.

Corbett tried to extract the testimony he wanted from a slightly different angle.

"Did Jean Powers die?"

"Yes," I replied.

"After she died, did you still carry out her verbal wishes regarding her beloved cat?"

"Yes I did."

"Why? She couldn't change her Will after she passed away?"

"I had met a Catholic priest on my holiday to Las Vegas and seeing what a quality human being he was made me question my own life."

The lead prosecutor yelled out an objection and demanded that both the question and answer be stricken from the record.

The Judge overruled the objection and advised Corbett to continue.

"Did your conduct as a lawyer change because of that encounter with the priest?"

"Definitely; I decided to retire in order to put an end to my disgusting greed, and I dropped my legal fees for each of the estates that I was in the process of administering."

Little Grey asked the next question.

"Did your new attitude cause you to be extremely generous with charities?"

I nearly answered in the affirmative, but I had decided to keep my recent gifts to the animal shelters completely secret from both Corbett and Timothy.

Although I felt that disclosing my generosity might influence the Judge to be lenient, somehow doing so didn't feel right. It was my prerogative to keep that part of my life unpublicized.

"Whatever I do with my money is my own business and certainly isn't relevant to how I may have deceived my clients."

The Judge spoke from behind the waterfall.

"Answer the question, Mr. Billingsworth."

My innate stubbornness took hold. I had been my own boss for my entire career and had never taken orders from anyone. I wasn't about to start now.

"I have answered the question, Judge."

"You don't appear to understand," his voice bellowed. "I'm ordering you to respond truthfully to the question you were asked by your own counsel."

I recalled my good sense when I first crossed the border into the USA at the beginning of my Las Vegas trip. I had wisely desisted from being rude to the customs agent. Now here I was getting sassy to someone who could do me serious harm, but I didn't care.

Not even some scary Judge was going to coerce me into giving away my right to privacy.

"I refuse to do so on the grounds that I can't be forced to provide an answer that may incriminate me."

Corbett interceded in an attempt to deflect the Judge's anger away from me.

"We have no further questions, Your Honor. The defense rests."

The courtroom was deathly silent for what seemed like an eternity.

Finally the Judge announced, "In light of the rebuttal evidence, I am reserving my decision in order to brush up on pertinent legal precedents. I will render my final decision in due course."

I woke up on Tuesday morning utterly confused about what had just transpired in the nightmare.

CHAPTER 30 (The Final Destination)

My two flights were both on time and when I reached Toronto I caught a bus back to Belleville.

The coach was almost full and a young woman sat down beside me.

We began chatting, and over the next hour she groaned about how difficult it was for youngsters her age to survive financially in this current economy.

She introduced herself as Alexia Quaterna, age 22, and she worked two part-time jobs, one in fast food and the other pumping gas.

Both positions paid minimum wage with no benefits, and if things were slow, she was often sent home early.

Alexia was returning from a medical appointment in Toronto. Unexpected prescription costs had drained her money three weeks ago and now she was six days late on her rental of a room in a Cobourg boarding house and in fear of being evicted.

There was something wrong with an affluent society like ours when a young woman with two jobs can't even make ends meet. I once believed that laziness or drug abuse caused poverty.

Spending so much time with Timothy had opened my eyes to the plight of ordinary hard-working folks who found themselves unable to cope with any emergency expense.

As we were pulling into the bus depot at Cobourg, I handed Alexia $1,000 in Canadian cash and wished her success in her future.

The look of pure relief in her face was delightful.

As the bus pulled away, I closed my eyes. It had been a rather grueling day of travel.

I must have dozed off because I found myself in another strange dream.

My furry pals Fluffy and Little Grey were trying to entice me to follow them down a winding rural path. In the distance I thought I caught a brief glimpse of Gabriela.

Before I could even get my bearings in the dream, I was jarred awake by the bus driver announcing that we had arrived at the downtown Belleville bus station.

A few other people got off the bus before me and hired the two available taxis.

I retrieved my luggage from the bus storage compartment and decided to walk the very short block to my building on Church Street.

I rested for a moment at the traffic lights and then lugged my loads across Bridge Street.

I walked past the large stone United Church which stood majestically next door to my office building.

Belleville had been my home all my life and I felt extremely comfortable here. So much about the city was so thoroughly familiar to me.

As I reached the sidewalk in front of my building, I stopped to admire how nice it looked with the new paint job.

I had made it safely back home.

At that precise moment I heard a commotion behind me and swung my head around to see what was causing the noise.

A delivery truck had lost control and mounted the sidewalk. It was about to crush me but I was frozen in place.

Pain engulfed me and then semi-darkness.

I felt paws touching me and I opened my eyes as I raised my head slightly.

It was Fluffy and Little Grey. I was lying on the ground and the cats each had hold of one of my arms and were tugging at the sleeves of my El Cortez jackpot sweatshirt.

I marveled at how strong they were. The little beasts were gently pulling me inch by inch down the same winding path I had just dreamt about.

As we slowly rounded a bend in the path, the darkness suddenly lifted and a bright loving light filled the universe.

Fluffy and Little Grey were now on my lap purring contentedly and Gabriela was tenderly caressing my face. She was so angelic.

I knew that I had arrived at my final destination where love was enveloping me.

THE END

www.ingramcontent.com/pod-product-compliance
Lightning Source LLC
Chambersburg PA
CBHW032116170626
46808CB00006B/1964